DARCY'S DECISION

Given Good Principles
Vol. 1

by

Maria Grace

Published by: Good Principles Publishing

Darcy's Decision

Copyright © 2012 Maria Grace

All rights reserved.

ISBN: 061558277X
ISBN-13: 978-0615582771

Author's Website: AuthorMariaGrace.com

Email address: Author.MariaGrace@gmail.com

GOOD PRINCIPLES
P U B L I S H I N G

DEDICATION

For my husband and sons who
have always believed in me.

ACKNOWLEDGMENTS

So many people have helped me along the journey to take this from an idea to a reality. Lisa, Matt and Debra Anne, thank you for being my original betas and cheering section. Linnea, Barb, Kathryn, Jan, and Gayle you've kept me going and helped more than I can say. And my dear friend Cathy whose interest and support kept me from chickening out more than once. Thank you!

1 TO WHOM MUCH IS GIVEN

Early spring, 1812

They are gone ...

The first fiery rays of daybreak blazed behind the marble cherubim guarding the graves. Despair contorted Fitzwilliam Darcy's face, threatening to defeat his last fragile threads of control. He gulped in the morning mist, fists balled, arms shaking. Ragged gasps tore from his chest; he opened his eyes and blinked the burning moisture away.

Backlit against the dawn, two headstones filled his view. The one on the right listed slightly, its inscriptions half-covered by a creeping vine that, come summer, would erupt in delicate white flowers. The other gravestone still stood solidly upright. The neat soil mounding before it bore no new growth though, if one looked closely, the barest signs of green were just becoming visible.

From a window of the nearby stone church, John Bradley contemplated the familiar vigil. He shrugged on his coat, fingers pausing over the threadbare patch at the elbow, and reached for his wide-brimmed hat. Cane in hand, he shuffled toward the heavy door. The chill wind buffeted him as he stepped into the morning.

They stood together silently, taking in the sunrise.

"Someday I must take my place here beside them." Shadows masked the inscriptions: GEORGE DARCY … DEPARTED THIS LIFE ANNO DOMINI 1811 … LADY ANNE DA— vines obscured the rest.

"I would prefer a situation in the shade. Over there, I think." Bradley pointed to a grassy spot near the church wall. "You cannot rid yourself of me, you know. I held you in my arms to baptize you into the church, and I will keep watch over you even from there."

Darcy chuckled, but his shoulders slumped, and he stared into his empty palms. "I miss him, Mr. Bradley. Father always knew what to do. Everyone trusted him." He rubbed the back of his neck, sighing out the emptiness that churned within. "I trusted him."

A cold gust blew through the graveyard. The iron gate clanged, the sound echoing against the stones.

"How can I take his place as master?" His guts twisted, the words burning his throat.

"Your father doubted himself, too."

"He did?"

"Many evenings, over tea, we talked of his misgivings." The corners of Bradley's mouth lifted and his eyes twinkled. "He had an excessive fondness for my cook's shortbread."

"He went to you to find wisdom. Father valued your advice and insight above all others."

Bradley dipped his head, blinking.

"I am not like him." Darcy grimaced and swallowed hard against the rising bile. "I lack his wisdom, his discernment."

"But you were given good principles, the ones your father stood on."

The wind whipped his coattails and scoured his face. "Are they enough?"

"He found them so." Bradley clapped his shoulder.

They locked in a penetrating gaze. Finally, Darcy released a deep breath. A slow smile spread but did not quite reach his eyes. "Join me for breakfast this morning? I must mediate a tenant quarrel today and need my father's wisdom."

"I would be honored."

They strolled to the manor, the gate jangling behind them.

•°꧁°꧂•°꧁°꧂••°꧁°꧂••°꧁°꧂••°꧁°꧂••

Late spring 1812

Darcy settled into the faded upholstery, drinking in the soothing scents of firewood, books, and leather.

The fireplace crackled and flickered hypnotically, mesmerizing him until a groaning creak disturbed his repose.

"Your father preferred that chair, too." Bradley laughed, shouldering the door open, a tray of tea and biscuits balanced in his hands.

"I remember sitting on this rug, looking at the picture books you kept in the basket by the fire." His fingers drifted across the frayed fabric.

"I still have those." Bradley parked the tray and turned to the bookcase. His hand hovered a moment, and he plucked a book from a haphazard stack. He gave it to Darcy, winking. "You amused yourself with them for hours while your father and I talked."

Darcy flipped through the pages, his fingertips tracing the pictures. Lips parted, he smiled, brushing his knuckles along his jaw. When he came to the end, he shut the book and helped himself to tea.

"The Good Lord willing, someday another generation of Darcys will play on my hearth rug." Bradley relaxed into his chair, propping his feet on the well-worn footstool. "So how did you find Rosings Park this year?" His teacup hid a mischievous smile.

"I would rather be here than in any of Rosings' well-fitted drawing rooms." He snorted and stretched his legs. "My aunt is much as she ever was."

"I have been honored by the distinguished lady's presence but twice. The first time, she advised me on how best to advance in the church. The second, she was decidedly put out because I had not followed her guidance."

"Be assured, your disobedience continues to disturb her ladyship to this day. She is not what you would call a forgiving soul." Darcy scooped up several pieces of shortbread. Reverently raising them to his lips, he caught the crumbs in his palm. "She cannot understand why you refused her offer."

Bradley's cup clacked softly against its saucer. He clasped his hands loosely and leaned forward on his knees. "I love this parish and its people. I cannot leave them any more than I could cut off my own legs." His eyes glittered. "A living, even at Rosings, is nothing to me."

"But taking the sinecure[1]—"

"—would mean leaving my people in a stranger's care."

"So you sacrificed yourself, giving up a secure future in favor of your parish, despite the fact you are merely a curate." Darcy scooped the last crumbs into his mouth, brushed his palms, and folded his arms across his chest. "Our *vicar*, Mr. Harris, never showed the parishioners such concern. He is at Kympton only as often as needed to fulfill the terms of the benefice,[2] yet he did not deign to allow you the use of the parsonage!"

---

[1] Sinecure : Church benefice to which no spiritual or pastoral charge is attached

[2] Benefice: or a "living," is used in the Church of England to describe a parish and its benefits including the church, parsonage house, and glebe (farm) land

"Harris is a good man, though, I admit, few call him friend. What he does is valuable. I am grateful he allows me to stay here instead of replacing me with someone younger and more like himself."

"That will not happen." The last violet rays of sunset caught Darcy's eyes as he tried to hide his scowl.

"I will not leave my parish. It is far too high a price for a living. My needs are well met as curate, thanks to a certain family's generosity," he winked, reaching for another biscuit, "and the Good Lord's grace."

Darcy rubbed his knuckles across lips that gathered into a frown. "Would you take Kympton if it were vacant?" He hunched forward and held his teacup, fixing on the amber liquid within. "I had a letter waiting for me on my return from Rosings." A heavy breath escaped. "Mr. Harris died a little over a week ago."

Bradley winced, the half-eaten shortbread forgotten in his grasp.

"While visiting with his sister in town, he took a cold that settled into his lungs. He declined rapidly, and it was just a matter of days. She and her son were at his side when he passed."

"I am glad he was not alone." Bradley removed his glasses and rubbed the back of his hand across his eyes.

A soft silence descended, punctuated by the popping fire and crunching biscuits. An unspoken demand hung in the air, filling the room with crackling tension.

"So, will you take Kympton now?" Darcy rested his chin on his fist and waited.

Bradley's shoulders bowed; he drummed his fingers and tapped his heel. Finally, he sprang up and wandered to the window. "It is a great deal more than I need."

"Have you not taught me, a worker is worth his wage?"

A wry smile slowly pulled at the corner of Bradley's lips. "So you have been listening." He braced himself on the windowsill, extending his legs, ankles crossed. "I will accept—" He held out his hand to restrain Darcy's enthusiastic response. "*However*, you must first demonstrate you are able to do more than repeat my lessons back to me. What have *you* done with that principle, and what have you seen come from it?" Crossing his arms over his chest, he leaned against the glass.

"Any other man would jump at the offer and be done with it." Darcy threw up his hands then laced them behind his head and stared into nothing.

Bradley shrugged.

"Well, there is an interesting conversation indeed. Let me count my benefits." He leaned forward, squeezing his temples with his elbows. "I have acquired Lady Catherine's contempt, for I allow you far too much influence." He threw his head high. His voice became shrill and nasal to match. "The lower classes put wealth to nefarious uses. Such means should be reserved for more noble purposes." Turning to the fireplace, he stroked his jaw. "Are the many long lectures from Lord Matlock to be considered among my gains? He warns me I will give away Pemberley's future." His chin fell and his shoulders squared. He inhaled hard and continued in a contrabass rumble, "Who are you, Fitzwilliam Darcy, to question tradition? How can Bradley condone such ideas? His sworn duty is to uphold the social order."

Forehead wrinkling, Bradley hurried to him. "What have you done?"

"After your eloquent preaching on the topic, I scoured the estate's books. Despite Father's goodness and benevolence, at the end, I found little difference between Rosings and Pemberley. He was not as liberal a master as I believed. So," he glanced up, "your admonishments ringing in my ears, I chose a different path."

Bradley pulled the footstool close and sat, his gaze not leaving Darcy.

"After collecting the rents at Michaelmas,[3] I purchased two seed drills, one for the home farm, and one for use among the leaseholders. After much research, and on the advice of Mr. Cooperton, I invested in new strains of livestock. The farmers may use the stud animals for one part in ten of their profits. Since my steward discovered many houses in need of major repairs, I did not increase their rents for the coming year."

"And the tenants response?" Bradley chewed his lip.

A lopsided grin gradually lit Darcy's face. "Well, a number of pub fights in Lambton have been credited to

---

[3] Michaelmas: September 29

my decisions." The smile broadened with the deepening creases on Bradley's brow. "I am told a villager criticized the Master of Pemberley, and several of our people took offense."

Bradley chortled, holding his belly.

"I cannot say anything for certain until the harvest; however, all signs point to profits well above my outlay. At least for now, it appears you were correct." Darcy's gaze drifted toward the window. "Uncle Matlock will credit quality seed and excellent weather for my success, not the work of good men."

"Lord Matlock holds to the traditional ideas of men and their worth."

Tension flooded Darcy's limbs, and he had to move. He jumped up and stalked along the fireplace. "My worthy uncle believes a man's birthright makes him significant. But what he produces of his own efforts is sullied because he has dirtied his hands."

"This troubles you?"

"Father taught me my worth came from being a Darcy, the next Master of Pemberley. He insisted that those of our circle were more important than anyone else." He stopped, grasped the mantle, dragged in several deep breaths, and then shoved himself away. "But such would not be the destiny of my dear playmate, George! No, being merely a steward's son, he will never suffer the high opinion of society." He clutched his temples and huffed. "I am certain Father wished George had been born *his* son." He kicked the rug and slouched against the bookcase. Head drooping, he searched the titles but found nothing.

Bradley grimaced.

"I am at a loss to understand. What makes a great man, Mr. Bradley?" He wrapped his arms around his chest, staring at the worn rug. "Back at Cambridge, I thought it right to measure him by the nobility of his line and the size of his estate. At school, I saw many heirs whose comportment put even George to shame. As long as no *respectable* woman was involved, their transgressions were overlooked for the sake of their family's name. Provided debts of honor were paid, debts to honest merchants could be ignored. What matter that their children would go hungry?" Shoulders falling, he paced again. "But nothing has the power to make a tradesman's son the equal of those curs."

"Now you question those values?"

Darcy hunched and looked away.

"You were born a Darcy. That makes you a better man than your tenant, Mr. Martin?"

"So I was taught."

"Perhaps," Bradley shuffled to his side, "you were born a Darcy because you lack the strength to have been born a Martin."

·•·❦◈·•·•·❦◈·•·•·❦◈·•·•·❦◈·•·•·❦◈·•·

Darcy pounded his pillow and flung himself onto his back for the hundredth time. Suddenly the blankets were too hot, tangled in his limbs, constricting. Fighting them off, he leapt from his bed. Frustration erupted in a snarl, and he wrenched open the window. The chill night air forced itself in, penetrating his thin nightshirt, quenching the burning in his chest. Braced against the casing, he rolled his forehead on the cool glass.

Not strong enough to be a Martin! He scanned the silvery landscape, all but seeing himself storm from Bradley's cottage. *A farmer, stronger than I?* He grumbled deep in his throat and threw the window shut with an empty clatter.

At first he searched for his dressing gown—a bit of brandy would surely settle his restlessness. No, a glance at the clock revealed dawn's impending arrival, and sleeping the day away was not an option. He reached for the bell, but his hand froze midway. *Am I a child who cannot dress himself? Must I call for another to fasten my buttons?* He ground his teeth painfully, stomping to the pile of clothes he had hastily shed not many hours before.

Storming from his chambers, he encountered servants scurrying about on their business. Their presence only managed to irritate him, driving him to plunge down the stairs two at a time. Fragrant aromas from the kitchen beckoned, promising comfort. He found none among the startled staff that bustled throughout the room. *My uncle and aunt both tell me I am an early riser, and yet the whole of Pemberly is at work before I awake.*

Chest constricting, he fled for refuge in the stables. A groom hurried to attend him, but Darcy's scowl frightened him off. He tore his saddle from the wall and breathed deeply. The scents of leather and horses and sweat filled him, anchoring him to the land, the one thing still unchanged. The familiar motions of readying his mount became a meditation; his heart slowed, and his mind began to clear.

He raced across the estate, momentarily aware of nothing but the wind in his face. Soon though, his thoughts strayed to the tenant farmers and craftsmen beginning their workdays—days filled with heavy, hard labor, dawn until dusk, only to trudge home for a meal and the opportunity to do it all again the next day. *I am told they are thankful to live in a place like Pemberley. Would I be grateful being a servant, not the master?*

The lopsided oak that marked his favorite copse emerged from the mist. *How did I get here?* The horse stopped at the narrow stream, and he dismounted. Still panting, he dropped onto a fallen log. The feathery moss under his fingertips gave him pause. *A far cry from the fine leather of my study.* Rolling his eyes, he tipped his head up, drawing in the smells of fresh water and loam.

Richard has spent many nights in places like this one … and worse. He has seen battle, held dying men, nearly died himself and more—things he will not speak of— because he is the second son. Had I an elder brother, would I have been there, too?

His belly rumbled painfully, and he scrubbed his face with his hands. *Have I ever missed a meal? Could I even prepare one? What am I without my staff to attend me?* He jumped up and stalked along the stream. The gushing waters struggled to keep up.

I studied under how many masters—to read, to write, for history, literature, and sums? They told me I was a man of sense and education. Yet I stand here wondering, if I took Richard's or Martin's place, would I do it half so well? How much sense do I possess?

A bird cawed overhead, answered by another and another until the branches erupted in a raucous conversation. The horse nickered, and a velvety black nose bumped his neck. *My peers say I am a superior equestrian, an excellent huntsman. But what good is it? Am I merely a child at play? Is Pemberley my nursery?* His stomach cramped, growling audibly. The stallion tossed his mane, ears pricked. He swung into the saddle. Shoulders sagging and eyes downcast, he let his mount carry him home.

Halfway to the house, Darcy saw several maids in the distance, lugging a rug outside, beaters in hand. Shaking his head sharply, he urged his horse away. Before he realized it, he was in the churchyard. He tied the stallion to an iron picket, noticing how the rust had been scoured away and fresh paint applied. His chest tightened, forcing muttered nothings from his lips, and he leaped the fence. He found the angel monument. Among the quiet graves, the warm rays of morning kissed his cheeks and blunted the edges of his turmoil.

"So you returned, despite your promise last night."

His ears burned, and he ran his fingers along the inside edge of his neck cloth. "I understand why my aunt chose her own vicar so carefully." A droll grin crept over his face.

"Indeed?" Bradley winked.

"It does not give the *ton* a good impression when one commits one's rector to Bedlam." He ignored Bradley's snicker. "My aunt would surely have done it had you spoken to her the way you did me yesterday." He lifted his brows over a tight smile.

Eyes twinkling, Bradley flung his head back and laughed heartily. He waved toward the cottage. "Would you join me to break your fast?"

Darcy's stomach grumbled loudly. Patting his belly, he guffawed. "Well, I suppose that prevents all prevarication. I will."

After breakfast, Darcy sank into his father's favorite chair. He smoothed his hair and covered his forehead with his arm, breathing deeply. "Thank you," he whispered.

"You are always welcome."

Darcy dragged his hand down his face. "You challenged all I have been taught about myself, who and what I am."

Bradley rested his elbows on the arms of his chair and laced his fingers.

"I need answers." His head lolled to the side, pulse throbbing in his ears. "It is your job as my vicar to—"

"Your vicar?"

"If the benefice is not filled soon, George Wickham will be at the door demanding it as the legacy my father promised him." He bit back bitter words that begged for voice.

"He has not taken orders yet." Bradley balanced his cheek on his knuckles.

"No, but he is only one bribe away from it."

"I have never had aspirations for wealth or situation. Now you are forcing me into a position where I must accept both." Bradley blew out a long breath.

"Perhaps in order for you to teach me what I am to do with my own."

Bradley sat up, staring at Darcy. The corners of his eyes wrinkled as he glared. A moment later, he began to laugh until tears flowed. *"Touché!"* He removed his glasses and wiped his eyes with the backs of his hands. "I will accept the living."

"At last!" The corner of his mouth twitching, Darcy propped his elbows on his knees. "Now tell me, how do I become the man my father wanted me to be?"

"Is that all you desire? I expected you to strive for more."

Darcy muttered under his breath, biting his upper lip to combat an angry retort.

Fingers drumming against his face, Bradley focused on the dust motes that danced in the sunbeam. "You have been given much; it brings heavy responsibility. Too few of your rank understand the concept."

"Father said I should keep and increase Pemberley, passing it on to my son to do the same."

"True enough, but think about the lives dependent on Pemberley. How many children grow up in the shadow of your decisions?" Arms braced against the chair, Bradley hoisted himself up and stood at the window. "If you aspire to be a truly excellent master, care for those who rely upon you. Are not the two greatest commandments to love God and to love thy neighbor?"

He cocked his head. "Who is my neighbor?"

Bradley studied him, chuckling softly. "I believe you are not the first to ask that question."

Darcy scowled, shifted several times in his seat, and rose. "My father and uncles insisted I protect our name, our legacy, and our reputation, valuing those above all else. Now *you* tell me my duty is to care for the people they declare insignificant." He rubbed his temples hard and propped his shoulder on the bookcase.

"I am afraid so." Bradley shrugged.

"Where do I begin?" He ran his hand down the shelves, ruffling papers. A loose sheet fluttered to the floor. "How will you manage your new-found wealth?"

Resting against the window, Bradley stared at the ceiling. "So many needs ... I must pray and seek the Almighty's wisdom to understand which are given me to meet. Perhaps you might help me evaluate them."

"What a change from your predecessor," he mumbled, snickering, and stooped to retrieve the fallen page.

Bradley fixed his somber eyes on him. "Work with me to serve and care for the least of your people. That is how you will be a truly great man."

2 BAD COMPANY CORRUPTS GOOD CHARACTER

Neck screaming and shoulders begging for release, Darcy pushed back from his work. A pained groan escaped when he hauled himself out of the chair. He shook away the tension and yawned. A careless stretch rattled his parents' portrait. He straightened it, hearing his mother's voice, *"You are all arms and legs son. Pay better attention!"* Warmth suffusing his chest, he gave the painting an affectionate brush and returned to his desk.

He cringed; letters and ledgers were strewn about, along with hastily scribbled notes and crumpled memos retrieved from coat pockets. *How did it become so unkempt?* His father's words rang in his ears, *"A good master keeps his work in order!"* "Yes sir," he whispered and set to repairing the disarray.

Satisfied at last, he removed bronze and marble paperweights from the drawer and placed them on the neat stacks. *I need air!* Quick steps carried him across the room to open the window. He drank in the fresh breeze. *Few sights are more satisfying than newly planted fields.*

Strains of piano music drifted in, occasionally interrupted by the bleating of sheep in the nearby pasture. He closed his eyes and allowed the serenity to envelope him. *I understand why Father loved the spring. I wish he were here to share it.* Memories of his parents filled his mind as he contemplated their portrait. *I am grateful for every day I had with him, though I would not relive those last three years.* He shuddered. Eyes wandering to the ceiling, he imagined his sister in the music room above. *How am I to raise a girl of fifteen?*

He raked his hair, hoping to comb away the pressure in his head. Failing, he rang for Mrs. Reynolds. Her distinct knock soon followed. "Come."

She shouldered the door open, carrying a tankard of fresh cider. "You have not stirred from this room all morning!"

A smile crinkled his cheeks when she pressed the fragrant beverage into his hand. "Thank you." He took a sip, and traced his steps back to his desk, sliding a stack of papers out of the way to accommodate the mug.

"You called for me, sir." Her eyes twinkled despite otherwise perfect decorum.

"I did." He set aside a horse-shaped paperweight and removed a pile of letters. "I wish you to read these."

She took the thick collection, squinting to decipher the topmost sheet.

"Mr. Bradley and I are seeking a teacher."

"Teacher, sir?"

"With no mistress at Pemberley, the education of the tenants' children has been neglected." He braced his elbows on the desk and laced his fingers. "Bradley lives in the parsonage now. His old cottage will become a school. First, we must find a teacher."

"You wish for me—"

"—to review those letters of character and give me recommendations." He smiled, noting the way her cheeks colored. "I need your evaluations by Saturday."

"Very good, sir." She curtsied and, seeing his nod, turned to leave. At the door, she paused and glanced over her shoulder. "You are the best of masters."

"Not yet, Mrs. Reynolds, but I am learning." *Uncle Matlock would be appalled! A waste of good resources, teaching tenants to read and write!* He reclined in his chair and laughed, looking over the home farm once again. A breeze rustled the papers on his desk, drawing his attention to them, and he began sorting letters. *Business. Business. A dinner ... that one to decline ... Ah! A letter from Bingley at last!*

Darcy,

I was so pleased to receive your invitation. You are right! A visit is long overdue.

My father's intention was to make me a gentleman. Though I am three and twenty, I yet feel unequal to the task of running an estate. Your tutelage will be most welcome. Are you certain preparing my sister to manage my household will not inconvenience your housekeeper too much?

I feel compelled to warn you, unlike myself, Caroline is actively seeking a marriage situation. Though you share much in common, please believe I am not trying to further a match between the two of you. While nothing would please me more than calling you brother, I prefer to leave matchmaking to the women.

Should you decide against her, I ask only that you tell her quickly and clearly, lest I endure her endless scheming. If you resolve in her favor, I beg you, forget I said that and never, ever speak of it.

Expect our visit on Tuesday, the last week in April, assuming, of course, the date is still agreeable to you.

CB

He arrives tomorrow! Darcy tossed the letter aside and pressed his forehead into the heel of his hand. *Why does this manner of confusion always ensue when Bingley is involved? How will he oversee an estate? He cannot even manage his own correspondence.* Sighing, he rang the bell. *Would Father have approved of Bingley's roots in trade?* Not pleased with the answer, he frowned and refolded the letter.

• • ❧❧ • • ❧❧ • • ❧❧ • • ❧❧ • • ❧❧ • •

Darcy jerked his sleeves and straightened his cravat while he waited for the approaching carriages. Thoughts of Miss Bingley floated through his mind, arousing his worst anxieties. *Then again, Bingley said we had much in common. Perhaps ...*

The first carriage lurched to a stop, and a well-dressed young man bounded out. "I say, Darcy, Pemberley does live up to your descriptions. I presumed you fanciful when you told me of it, but indeed, you were not! This is the most remarkable place!" He grinned, whipping his head around to take in everything at once, ginger curls bobbing wildly.

"I am glad you are come. Although I must admit, you had my staff scrambling. Your letter arrived only yesterday."

"Yesterday?" Charles rubbed his chin. "Are you certain?"

"You should give your penmanship greater attention. You wrote the direction most ill indeed." Darcy glared but knew his friend recognized the glint of mischief in his eye.

"Yes, well, we are here now, if, of course, you do not choose to turn us out."

"That is an option, I suppose, one I will not rule out for the time being."

"Then I will be certain to stay on my best behavior." Bingley laughed and handed his sister out of the carriage.

The first thing Darcy noted was her gown. Though the sarsanet[4] finery demonstrated her superior taste, the dress suited neither her nor the business of traveling. He tugged at his neck cloth.

"May I present my sister, Miss Caroline Bingley."

Darcy bowed. "Welcome to Pemberley."

"Thank you, Mr. Darcy." She batted her eyelashes.

Darcy pressed his lips tightly, the knot in his belly growing.

"My brother told me of you." Caroline stepped closer. "I have anticipated spending time in the company of someone so like-minded."

Retreating slightly, Darcy gestured toward the house. "My staff will show you to your rooms. You may refresh yourselves, and afterwards we will gather for tea."

"I can imagine nothing I would enjoy more than getting out of these dusty things." Charles started bounding up the stairs, but Caroline restrained him with a sharp cough.

"Charles, will you not lend me your arm before you dash off in a fury?"

The two men exchanged glances. Darcy cleared his throat, eyebrows raised.

---

[4]Sarsanet- a type of light silk

Bingley shrugged and escorted his sister into the house.

"Pemberley manor does you credit, Mr. Darcy. I always say a man's home tells a great deal about him." Her eyes darted around the foyer.

"Yes, she reminds me of that rather often," Charles laughed, "especially whilst instructing me on the intricacies of fine taste."

Caroline winced.

Darcy looked from one sibling to the other and tried not to fidget. "I am afraid I did not realize you would be here when planning tonight's dinner. Several of my neighbors are joining me for an evening honoring our new vicar."

"Your vicar?" She tilted her head, eyes narrowing. "What an odd occasion to celebrate."

Bingley held up a warning finger, but she ignored him.

"How magnanimous, giving a clergyman such notice!" She edged closer, fluttering her lashes.

"In truth, Miss Bingley, I find myself grateful for his attentions to me." Darcy stood a little straighter, back stepping slightly.

An agitated footman rushed to his side.

"Yes, Stevens, what is it?" He tried to hide his relief.

"Mr. Darcy, Mr. Wickham just arrived, sir." Deep creases lined Stevens's face.

Darcy gritted his teeth to contain the epithet that threatened to explode. "You may show him to my study." He clasped his hands behind his back and turned to his guests. "I am afraid I will not be able to join you for tea. I have an appointment that cannot be delayed. Refreshments will be sent to your chambers, and then my housekeeper can give you a tour until I am free."

"How kind of you, sir. A tour would be most agreeable." Miss Bingley beamed and gazed into his eyes.

He bowed, waving his staff into action. As he walked away, he snuck a final peek at Caroline. *How does Bingley consider us similar?* He shoved the disconcerting thought aside, realizing he had much bigger issues awaiting his attention.

⁕·ᕲᕗᕲ·⁕·ᕲᕗᕲ·⁕·ᕲᕗᕲ·⁕·ᕲᕗᕲ·⁕·ᕲᕗᕲ·⁕

Darcy paused before he reached the study. Tipping his head, he pinched the bridge of his nose and drew a deep breath. Once the edges of his irritation dulled, he cracked the door open to see George Wickham standing at the window. *I know that expression. He is scheming again.* A fresh wave of tension washed over him. *I am tired of rescuing him.*

Wickham strode to the desk and rifled through papers. A moment later, he had thrown open several drawers and was scanning the pages of a red leather-bound ledger.

Blood boiling, Darcy burst into the room. "Explain yourself!"

"Just a habit of my father's coming out, old friend. Your desk is a fright." He shook his head and tossed the ledger aside.

"Your father was an honorable man. He did not go sifting through another man's papers!" Eyes blazing, his fists quivered at his sides. "I should toss you out!"

"Temper, temper." Wickham waved him down. "So touchy today. What happened? Did your favorite horse turn up lame?"

"What do you want Wickham?" Darcy jostled past. "Have you ever arrived on my doorstep without a list of demands? Creditors come knocking? Or gambling debts this time?"

"What a low opinion of me! What would your father say?" Wickham draped himself over a nearby chair.

His eyes narrowed. "What would he say of your gaming companions running you out of town?"

"How long will you carry a grudge over a bit of harmless fun—"

"Your harmless fun nearly cost me—"

"Cost you nothing! Your connections insure—"

"That is not the point!" Darcy slammed the desk, his palms stinging against the polished mahogany.

Wickham smirked. "Relax, Darcy."

Teeth clenched, he wrestled the urge for violence into submission and snarled, "Why are you here? My patience is wearing thin."

"Did I hear correctly? Pemberley's dutiful son and heir disregarded his father's dearest wish and gave the old curate the living promised to me?"

"It was hardly his fondest desire." Darcy gripped the edge of the desk, certain he was leaving impressions in the wood.

"You deny he wanted me to have Kympton?"

"It is irrelevant. You are not even eligible to serve as a curate."

Wickham brushed the objection aside. "It is easily remedied."

"You intend to take orders? Would it not severely alter your lifestyle?"

"In exchange for the life of a gentleman's son, taking orders seems like a small thing. Besides, I do not see that so very much would be in need of change."

The image of Wickham in the pulpit flashed through Darcy's mind. He wrapped an arm across his churning belly. "It makes no difference. The living belongs to John Bradley now."

"You ignored your father's plans. That means nothing to you?"

Darcy's features hardened. "Father gave you no promises. Remember, I was the executor of his will. Had he intended to give you Kympton, he would have left you the advowson[5] thus allowing you to appoint yourself to the living." He pushed back, crossing his arms. "But he did not."

Eyes wide, Wickham shifted uncomfortably in his seat. "He told me clearly—"

---

[5] Advowson: right of presenting a clergyman to a living, viewed as a form of property. Some clergymen owned advowsons and could lawfully appoint themselves to a living

"He said he hoped you would take orders that you might be given Kympton someday. That can hardly be construed as a promise."

"You owe me the value of the living!" Wickham slapped the desk, nostrils flaring. "Three thousand pounds at least!"

"So, it is about money." Darcy slammed the drawer Wickham opened shut.

"I need help to get started. Your father—"

"He left you a thousand pounds in his will! The interest alone should have been sufficient—"

"Can you not forgive the indiscretions of youth?"

"Good Lord, Wickham! Less than a year?"

"I have learned my lesson." Wickham rose and trudged wearily to the window.

Is that possible? Darcy rubbed his thumb across his fingertips.

"I finally understand the love your father lavished on me, the undeserving offspring of his steward." He braced against the windowsill, back bowed. Wickham dropped his chin to his chest. "I wasted what he gave me, and I admit it. I beg you! Give me another chance. Does not your vicar teach of forgiveness? Am I not the prodigal son, returning to the fold?"

The rising warmth in Darcy's chest cooled instantly. "What do you know of his teachings? I do not remember you darkening Bradley's door."

"As if you have spent so much time there yourself." Wickham scoffed, pausing at the livid fire flashing in Darcy's eyes. He threw his head back and laughed.

"You, a church mouse? Has Bradley made you into a religious man? Will I be invited to your japanning?[6] Are you eyeing the living for yourself after Bradley's passing?"

Pushing off the desk, Darcy rose to his full height. "This interview is at an end, Mr. Wickham."

"No! Please." He rushed to Darcy's side. "Help me this time, and I will never come to you again. On my honor."

Darcy chewed his cheek and glanced toward the locked drawer containing his bank orders. An odd check in his guts stayed him. *Three thousand is not an insignificant sum.* "I will consider your request."

"Thank you—" He offered his hand.

"I said I would entertain the thought, nothing more. Do not thank me yet." Darcy glowered.

He edged away. "Have I heard correctly that you are hosting a dinner tonight to celebrate your new vicar? May I join you? I would like to congratulate the man who is filling my … uh … the living."

A sigh pooled in Darcy's throat, finally erupting as a distinct grumble. "All right, however, do not expect a guest room prepared for you."

"I took rooms in Lambton and shall not importune you further." He bowed stiffly and left, the corner of his lips rising.

•• ᏚᏬᏩᎥ •• ᏚᏬᏩᎥ •• ᏚᏬᏩᎥ •• ᏚᏬᏩᎥ •• ᏚᏬᏩᎥ ••

---

[6] Japanned: ordained, to put on black cloth; from the color of black japanware

"George! I thought I heard your voice! I am so happy to see you! Have you seen my brother yet?" She beamed, racing down the stairs to meet him.

"Georgiana!" Wickham caught her hands.

She giggled and blushed at his hesitance in releasing her. Her fingers tingled in the wake of his grasp.

"You are quite the lady now." His eyes drifted up and down in unhurried appraisal.

She blushed under his appreciative study.

"I should like to take a turn about the grounds with you, for old time's sake. What say you?" He offered his arm.

"I must ask my brother. He is awfully strict …" She frowned, a pinching ache beginning in her chest.

"Do you truly believe he would mind?"

"Well … you used to take me for walks … you and me and Fitzwilliam and Richard …" She bit her lower lip.

"Those were certainly halcyon days for us all." He looked away, eyes unfocussed. "How could he object to us reliving those moments for just a little while?"

"You are right. He would not refuse me." She bounced on her toes. "But I must watch the time. I have been permitted to join them at dinner tonight. My first evening in company!" She twirled and hugged herself. "Brother says this is a special honor, and I cannot be late."

"Of course. We will mind the minutes!" He escorted her to the gardens. "You have blossomed into an exquisite woman, my dear."

She tittered, her face growing hot. "Fitzwilliam does not seem to think so."

"What? Has he criticized your beauty? I will call him out!" He crossed his arms, scowling dramatically.

"No! No!" Georgiana laughed, touching his forearm. "It is just that he does not see me as a lady, not yet."

"I truly understand." Wickham squeezed her fingers. "To him, I am no gentleman."

"Oh, George! What happened?" Her head snapped up, her fingertips grazing the front of her neck.

"A gentlewoman should not listen to such troubles." Tucking her hand into his elbow, he walked on.

"No, please tell me. Perhaps I can do something."

"What an innocent. The sad truth is your brother has always been envious of me." He shook his head, lips drooping. "It is not proper for me to tell you such things. Forgive me—"

She stopped, tugging him closer. "Jealous?"

"It is wrong of me to criticize him before you."

"I am almost a woman. I should know these things!" Teeth gritted, she huffed and stomped. "Tell me!"

"He resented sharing your father's affection. Now, he denies me what your father promised me. He gave my living to the curate, leaving me penniless."

She clutched his hands, her eyes swimming with tears. "I cannot believe him so mean-spirited. I will talk to him and make him understand." Her belly twisted when he returned her wide-eyed gaze.

"You leave such worries to me. Tonight is your first dinner! I am excessively pleased to be able to join you.

Your brother has permitted me that much. Tell me everything—who is invited, what you are to wear. Let your good fortune distract me from my troubles." He blinked and forced a smile.

3 FROM THE OVERFLOW OF THE HEART THE MOUTH SPEAKS

Darcy huffed, pacing the room and tugging his cravat. *Who decided this torture device, disguised as fashion, was a good idea?* He worried the offending garment, eventually forcing himself to stop and straighten the white silk. *What a fool I was to give in to Wickham! No one wants his company tonight.* The chair by the fireplace groaned as he sprawled across it.

How does Wickham always manage to get what he wants? He stabbed the fire with the poker. His eyes followed the sparks as they rose. *Am I spiteful for not wanting to give him more money?* Grumbling, he stirred the flames once more and tossed the poker aside. Cross words cavorted along the edge of his tongue, but he restrained them and heaved himself up to stretch. *He is good at escaping the merchants, but his gaming companions must be tired of his evasions.* "Meh!"

A breeze drew his gaze to the window. His feet followed, and he leaned on the windowsill, looking over his estate. George Darcy's words rang in his ears. *"Never wager, son. We depend on the land for our survival; is that not gamble enough?"*

"It is indeed, Father," Darcy murmured. "Did Bradley teach you that?" He pulled the clattering pane closed and walked past the mirror to check the damage to his valet's careful knots. "I grieve to think of what you would say of your favorite's debts of honor."

· • ❦•❧ · • · ❦•❧ · • · ❦•❧ · • · ❦•❧ · • · ❦•❧ • ·

Darcy took a turn about the empty drawing room, appreciating the meticulous care his staff took in making sure each treasured object was in place, perfectly free from dust. *I must remember to give Mrs. Reynolds my compliments.* Uncluttered and elegant, the room's serenity washed over him, relieving some of his tension.

"Mr. Darcy!" Caroline swept in. Her pale peach, sarsanet gown rustled while the feathers on her turban bobbed in time.

Bingley peeked over her shoulder. "Good evening, Darcy!"

Darcy choked on his laughter, the image of a hound puppy flushing a quail from the underbrush clear in his mind. "Good evening." He schooled his features into a more proper expression. "I trust you found your accommodations acceptable?"

"Acceptable? You are indeed too modest." Caroline sidled closer. "I can hardly imagine better rooms."

"They are extremely fine! And the prospects ... such landscapes!" Bingley gestured toward the window.

"I am glad they were to your liking." He inclined his head, edging away.

"How do you manage not to get lost?" Bingley grinned and craned his neck to scan the corridor. "I made certain to count the doors to be sure I could find my way again!"

The men laughed, but Caroline's jaw dropped. She planted her hands on her hips. "Charles, how can you say such a thing?"

A careless wave brushed her off. "Darcy recalls my penchant for misdirection. Remember—"

"—you dragged me into town on the promise of finding the rare book seller?" Darcy crossed his arms lightly, a wry smile emerging.

"Indeed! We ended up ..." He glanced at his sister, cringing. "Ah ... we ... ah ..."

"Quite lost, and in unexpected places." Darcy's eyebrows twitched.

Caroline began to speak but was cut short by Stevens's appearance.

"Sir, Mr. Wickham." The burly footman bowed and stepped aside.

Darcy was certain he was being strangled and tugged at his cravat. To his surprise, it was no tighter than only a moment before. "Mr. and Miss Bingley, Mr. George Wickham."

Bingley covered his gaping mouth and looked to Darcy, who frowned briefly and shook his head.

"Madam," Wickham stepped forward, bowing over her proffered hand. "What a surprise to find Darcy entertaining such enchanting guests."

Caroline fluttered her eyelashes. "You are too kind, sir. Is your estate nearby?"

"No, Darcy and I grew up together—"

Nostrils flaring, Darcy glowered. "He is the son of my father's most trusted steward."

Wickham scowled and tipped his head. "Alas, the shameful truth of my birth is out."

"There is no disgrace in that! Our own father was in trade!" Bingley's face colored.

"He wished better for his children." Caroline tossed her head, her feather bouncing wildly, and glared at Bingley. "Are you seeking to purchase an estate, Mr. Wickham?"

He closed his eyes briefly. "My father had no riches to leave me. I am destined to work for my fortune. I would have liked to take orders and settle in the living old Mr. Darcy promised his favorite godson."

Darcy took a deep breath, balling his fist until his fingers ached. Stevens ushered in several more guests before he could give voice to the tense words that lodged in his throat. Shaking his revulsion aside, he hurried to the doorway.

"Mr. and Miss Bingley, may I present Mr. and Mrs. Cooperton and Mr. and Miss Lackley. They are my neighbors." His hackles raised at the mercenary gaze Wickham bestowed on Rebecca Lackley. He rubbed the back of his neck, wondering if anyone else noticed.

Cooperton extended his hand to Bingley. "How do you know Darcy, sir?"

"We attended Cambridge together. He took me under his wing and helped me make my way."

Caroline gave him a black stare.

"He is his father's son," Cooperton laughed a warm, friendly laugh, his ample belly shaking, "seeking to support the younger men."

"You knew the late Mr. Darcy well?" Lackley's blonde hair fell across his face, and he tossed it back.

"We were more than simply neighbors. He, Nathan King, the former owner of your estate, Edwards and I, we were tight." A half smile drew up the corners of Cooperton's mouth. "Those were good days."

"Dear Anne and sweet Marian," Mrs. Cooperton fanned herself with her handkerchief, "they were truly elegant ladies. Nevertheless, they knew every need on all our estates. Not a sick child ever missed their care. Such dear, dear friends." She dabbed her eyes.

"Was it not the King's estate—" Darcy asked.

"Yes." Cooperton rubbed his chin, turning to Lackley. "About twenty years ago, a terrible fire at Dunmore destroyed the west wing of the manor house, the main barn, and three out buildings."

"What an awful thing—they lost several servants and their two youngest children! Poor Marian was devastated!" Mrs. Cooperton blinked rapidly, eyes glistening. "Your father," she looked directly at Darcy, "and Mr. Bradley were there almost as soon as the alarm sounded. They rushed into the burning house to rescue two of the children and their nursery maids."

"It was by the Almighty's Grace that any of us escaped."

They noticed Bradley standing in the doorway, flanked by Edwards and a flustered Stevens.

Darcy dismissed the footman. "Mr. Bingley, Miss Bingley, this is our vicar, Mr. Bradley and Major, or as it is now, Mr. Edwards."

Edwards bowed to Caroline then turned and extended his hand to Bingley. "Darcy has spoken often of you, Mr. Bingley."

"Mr. Cooperton was telling us of the fire at Dunmore," Rebecca said, a light blush creeping over her cheeks. Her pale blonde hair was coiffed befitting a young woman just now out in society. A single curl escaped to grace the nape of her neck.

"Yes, I remember." Edwards pursed his lips. "What a tragedy." He clapped Bradley's shoulder. "Would have been much worse had it not been for you and Old Darcy. Neither of you ever took credit for saving those young ones."

Bradley shrugged. "It was the Good Lord's hand alone."

"As I recall, a couple of strong backs were involved as well." Edwards snorted and shared a somber look with Cooperton.

"Those were dark days for us all. The loss of a child is not something one overcomes easily." Bradley stroked his chin. "But, we carried one another through."

"We were more brothers than friends, no? Born for adversity, I believe you would say." Cooperton nudged Bradley.

Across the room, Wickham rubbed a finger along the side of his nose and shuffled his feet.

"It seems you do not agree, Mr. Wickham." Cooperton slowly walked toward him, the group parting to give him way.

Wickham swallowed hard and licked his lips. "In my experience, such friends are rare."

"Indeed, they are." Bradley stepped between Cooperton and Wickham. "But let us not dwell on such thorny matters now."

"Always a fount of wisdom, my friend." Cooperton leveled a warning look on Wickham and, with Bradley, returned to the larger group.

Bradley offered his hand to Bingley. "A pleasure to be introduced at last."

"Indeed it is, sir. Darcy has told me so much of you. I feel as though I already know you!" He pumped the vicar's arm.

Mrs. Reynolds signaled from the doorway. Darcy hastened to meet her and saw his sister standing beside her.

"Good evening, Brother." Georgiana lifted her face shyly, a flush of excitement brightening her cheeks.

"You are lovely tonight." *My little sister is a young woman now?* His stomach knotted at her innocent anticipation. Swallowing hard, he took her elbow and led her into the room. "Miss Bingley, may I introduce my sister, Miss Georgiana Darcy."

Georgiana curtsied. "I am pleased to meet you."

"The pleasure is mine, Miss Darcy." Caroline dipped gracefully. "What a lovely gown! White dimity[7] is most flattering."

"She is right, my dear," Mrs. Cooperton said, patting Georgiana's shoulder. "We are very pleased you will join us for dinner. Might we expect you to play for us afterwards?"

Georgiana wrung her hands. "I have never played for such a large group."

Rebecca took her arm. "I will turn the pages for you and help you find courage!"

"I am sure you will be able to play." Darcy smiled at the young ladies, although the tightness in his chest nearly stole away his breath.

"Excuse me." Rebecca pulled Georgiana toward the window. "I am overwhelmed by so much company! I

---

[7]Dimity: firm cotton fabric woven with a small raised pattern or stripe.

feel much better now that you are here, even if you are not yet out! I hope your brother allows us to sit close enough to talk at dinner." She glanced at Darcy.

"Mrs. Reynolds took pity on me and told me he gave her instructions to seat us together." Her eyes drifted toward Wickham who stood alone in the far corner.

"Why do you pine for him? He is a steward's son!"

"My brother has treated poor George cruelly!" Georgiana's brow knit.

"Do you realize—"

"It is time for dinner." Darcy beckoned them toward the doorway.

Bradley hurried over and extended his arm to Georgiana. She took it, but peeked at Wickham. Bradley followed her gaze and offered Wickham a cautionary look. Darcy escorted Mrs. Cooperton while Lackley attended Caroline. Bingley accompanied Rebecca, leaving Wickham to walk alone.

While they entered, servants placed platters on the mahogany table. Tempting aromas filled the air. Candlelight glittered throughout the dining room, sparkling off the mirrors and polished silverware.

"This is the kind of table your dear mother used to set. You do them proud." Mrs. Cooperton patted his hand. "They would have honored this occasion, too."

"Thank you." Darcy dipped his head.

"How elegant!" Caroline gasped, pausing to take it all in.

Darcy directed Mrs. Cooperton to the place of honor, beside him at the head of the table, and gestured

Bradley to his other side. Mrs. Reynolds arrived to guide Georgiana and Rebecca into adjacent seats, midway down. Cooperton and Edwards struck up a brief conversation with Wickham. After they finished, the only open chairs were well way from the unmarried ladies.

"Will our new vicar bless the meal?" Darcy asked.

Disapproval flashed in Georgiana's eyes. Wickham smiled tightly.

Bradley bowed his head, his rich baritone filling the room. "We thank You, our Heavenly Father, for friends and family and food. Your Grace has allowed us to gather to celebrate Your Goodness to us all. We are humbly grateful. Amen."

A brief silence followed, broken by Cooperton's chuckle. "Once again you demonstrate why we hold you in such high esteem! What is not to love about a short-winded clergyman?"

Caroline wrinkled her nose and turned aside while the rest laughed, Bradley loudest of all.

"You may laugh, Cooperton," Bradley grinned and shook his finger at the group, "but I am reminded of an important lesson I learned at Cambridge."

"And what would that be, sir?" Bingley asked.

"A man of too many words is usually a man of too little sense."

"Mr. Bradley!" Mrs. Cooperton giggled.

"I have heard even a fool is thought wise, if he keeps silent." Bingley served the ladies beside him from the nearby dishes.

"Indeed!" Cooperton chuckled and clapped Bingley's shoulder.

"Charles!" Caroline scowled. "My brother means no insult—"

"None taken, Miss Bingley, I assure you." Bradley waved her off. "He is quite correct. The more one speaks, the more likely he is to find he has said too much."

"A man is only as good as his word, is he not?" Darcy placed a slice of beef on Mrs. Cooperton's plate.

"Your father often said that." Cooperton winked at Bradley and waggled a finger at Darcy. "In fact, I remember when you were just a young man ..."

Darcy's face grew hot. "No, sir." He raised an open hand. "While I am host at this table, we will not review my boyhood foibles!" Although his words were stern, his eyes sparkled.

Georgiana leaned toward Rebecca and whispered, "How can he insult my brother in our home!"

"Dearest, you are too easily distressed. Why must you take offense on behalf of others?" She touched Georgiana's forearm. "They are only joking."

"It is not correct to make jests about their host." Georgiana turned away, pouting.

"Your brother does not seem to mind. He is smiling."

"His behavior is not so proper, either." She crossed her arms tightly around her waist. "He is ignoring poor George."

"Mr. Wickham sits near the foot of the table! Calling across such distances would be rude!" Rebecca replied through clenched teeth.

"So, Wickham, what brings you into our neighborhood after your long absence?" Edwards asked.

"I received the news Mr. Harris had passed." He looked away.

"You came to pay your respects?" Lackley dabbed his chin with his napkin.

"No, he did not."

Everyone gasped, staring at Georgiana.

"Stop it!" Rebecca hissed, reaching for Georgiana's hand.

"He was promised the living given to Mr. Bradley."

A hush fell over the table. Darcy's pulse thudded in his temples as the blood drained from his face. Jaw tense, he ground his teeth to avoid voicing sentiments he might later regret. No acceptable words offered themselves, so the breath he drew to speak escaped as indistinct mumbles.

Bradley pitched forward over the table, trying to catch Georgiana's attention. "My dear, Mr. Wickham has not yet taken orders. That means the living would remain vacant for rather a long time."

"I do not believe it a very bad a thing that the parish should be without a cleric for a time." Georgiana looked at the napkin she was twisting on her lap. Crimson rose along her neck and over her ears, tingeing her cheeks.

Wickham coughed into his hands, but Darcy noticed his satisfied expression.

"Except for Sundays, what does the vicar do?" Georgiana did not lift her eyes while she spoke. "Mr. Harris was every bit the idle gentlemen. He hired Mr. Bradley to manage the parish and someone else to farm the glebe.[8] Oh, occasionally, he would visit the sick and console with the old, but Mrs. Cooperton does that too. Is it so troubling for someone else to attend those duties for a time?" Her shoulders twitched. "As for reading sermons—"

"Georgiana!" Darcy's booming voice rattled the chandelier's crystals.

"It is all right." Bradley took in the horrified expressions around the table.

"No, sir, it is not. Clearly, being in company is too much excitement for her." Darcy rose slowly, glowering at his sister.

She blanched, and her lower lip quivered.

"You may return to the nursery. I will speak to you in the morning."

Tears sprang to her eyes. She jumped to her feet and fled.

"Please, forgive my sister." Darcy sank into his seat, his stomach soured.

"Do not trouble yourself on my account. The young are not always conscious of what they say." Bradley nodded.

---

[8] Glebe: the farmable land associated with a parish church or living

Cooperton shared a meaningful gaze with his wife.

Wickham fixed his attention on his plate, unsuccessfully hiding a thin smile.

Darcy rang the bell. Servants appeared to clear off the dishes from the first course and bring in the second. Some of the tightness in the back of his neck dissipated when new conversations began in their wake.

"Mr. Darcy," Caroline's nasal voice prickled along his spine, "your table is remarkably elegant. Who plans your menus for you?"

For once, he welcomed the inane question. "Mrs. Reynolds, my housekeeper. She has been a part of this household since I was a child and was my mother's most trusted aid."

"Anne set such a beautiful table for her guests. Mrs. Reynolds keeps her ways alive and well despite her being gone all these years. The influence of a good mistress lingers long in her absence." Mrs. Cooperton watched Caroline carefully.

"I believe my sister anticipates serving as mistress of my estate," Bingley said. "I expect she would like to set a table as fine as this someday."

"You recently purchased property?" Lackley squared his shoulders. "I have lately bought mine."

"Not yet, but I hope soon." Bingley grinned. "I thought myself in the company of old landed families like Darcy's."

"If only that were so! It was my father's dying wish…"

"Likewise my own!" Bingley slapped the table. "A kindred spirit indeed!"

"You and Lackley have much in common." Darcy looked from one to the other. "I believe his insight might prove valuable to you this season."

"Always watching out for me, Darcy! I should very much like to talk to you, Lackley."

"You must come to tea and tour Dunmore! Perhaps even stay a day or two." Lackley nodded at Rebecca. "What say you, in two days? Give my sister a chance to practice as hostess herself."

"I would be honored for your company, sir." Rebecca cocked her head. "Perhaps Miss Bingley might join you too?"

Startled, Caroline took a moment to reply. "Yes, certainly, thank you." She glanced from Darcy to Lackley while the servants cleared the second course, brought in dessert, and poured sweet wine.

Darcy raised his glass. "A toast to our faithful friend: May his wisdom guide yet another generation in Derbyshire."

"To Bradley."

The man himself squirmed slightly, a bright flush creeping along his jowls.

A lively conversation ensued regarding the relative merits of cake over pie. After generous samples of both, Darcy slid his chair back. "Shall we all repair to the drawing room?"

4 FOLLY IS BOUND UP IN THE HEART OF A CHILD

His guests lingered in the dining room for a few more moments. Darcy wasted no time seeking Wickham who was conversing with Miss Bingley.

Her visage brightened at Darcy's approach. "What a lovely meal, sir. I do hope your sister's departure did not disrupt plans for the gentlemen to share port and cigars in the dining room. I would be most happy to attend to the ladies—"

"Not at all, madam. My intentions were for the entire party to withdraw together." Though he spoke to her, his eyes focused on Wickham.

"What, no port? Uncivilized!" Wickham folded his arms across his chest, laughing.

Beneath his too-tight cravat, Darcy's neck twitched. "Then you have nothing to repine since you will be leaving us directly."

"Excuse me?" Wickham cocked his head and stared down his nose.

The temperature between the two men plummeted. Caroline shivered and rubbed her arms briskly. "Oh, I just remembered, I must ask Miss Lackley ..." She dropped a brief curtsey and hurried away.

"It is time for you to go." Darcy cut off Wickham's words with his hand and waved toward the doorway.

Wickham blew out a deep breath through puffed cheeks. "You are correct. Thank you for your hospitality."

Darcy followed him to the foyer. The butler dodged to permit Darcy to open the door himself. Wickham bowed, offered effusive farewells, and left.

"Do not allow him in again." Darcy glared at his man, knowing the servant did not deserve his ire.

"Absolutely, sir. I shall inform the rest of the staff." He bowed.

Darcy nodded and watched him hurry off. For a moment, he considered retreating to his study, but immediately dismissed the idea. Halfway back to his guests, he paused, squeezing his temples. Relief wrestled with ire and mortification. His sister's words still rang in his ears. *How did Wickham influence her so quickly?*

A quarter of an hour in the parlor, listening to his friends' conversations, soothed Darcy's ragged temper. At length, he excused himself and strode to the pianoforte opposite the fireplace.

He played a loud chord and waited until the room stilled. "Mr. Bradley, one of Father's fondest wishes was for you to be appointed to Kympton. He purchased this," Darcy removed a violin from the bench, "in anticipation of this day." He beckoned Bradley close and placed it in his hands while their friends softly applauded.

"He remembered," Bradley whispered. Eyes bright, his fingertips caressed the finely polished wood and taut strings. "Many years ago, I had such an instrument, but hard times forced me to sell it. Your father, though cross I did not seek his help first, promised to find a way to restore it to me." He blinked hard. "Thank you."

"Now you must honor us and play," Edwards said, turning to the others.

"Hear, hear!" Cooperton clapped from his seat near the fireplace.

Darcy retrieved a folio of music from the pianoforte bench and pressed it into Bradley's hands, smirking.

Bradley chuckled. "I can hardly remember the last time these old digits graced the strings. You may well regret your polite demands." He rifled through the music. "This one looks familiar."

"Shall I turn pages for you?"

"I would welcome it. That way, you may take it from me before my performance becomes unbearable."

Bradley winked, tuning the instrument. He drew the bow and grimaced, retuned a string and tried again. This time he nodded at Darcy. Tucking the violin under his chin, he lifted the bow and began to play. Softly at first, then with increasing confidence, the sweet melody filled the room.

The last notes faded away, leaving a peculiar longing in their wake. Darcy swallowed the lump in his throat. *You chose a fitting gift, Father.*

"Thank you." Raising his glasses, Bradley scrubbed the back of his hand across his eyes.

Edwards stood, applauding. "Play us another!"

"Only if you come and sing." Bradley waved him forward.

Edwards shook his head, while the Coopertons grinned enthusiastically. "All right, I will take the bass line. We need a tenor, too." He glanced over the music Bradley pushed at him and pointed his chin at Cooperton.

"You know full well, I sound like a hound baying at the moon!" Cooperton turned to his wife and laughed.

"I sing a bit." Bingley rose despite Caroline's scowl.

Darcy noticed her disapproval and frowned at her display. *What was she expecting?*

Turning his back on her, Bingley strolled to Bradley and Edwards.

• • ❧ ❧ • • ❧ ❧ • • ❧ ❧ • • ❧ ❧ • • ❧ ❧ • •

"You may return to the nursery." Darcy's voice reverberated in her ears. Her face aflame, Georgiana fled. *How could he dismiss me? I am not a child. I have every right to sit with company! Mr. Bingley and Mr. Lackley do not exclude their sisters!* She paced before the staircase.

Rebecca is hostess for her brother's company. She is but a year and a half older than I. She stomped her slippered foot, ignoring the sting from the marble tiles. *I will not go upstairs!* A sob caught in her throat. *Father would have expelled Fitzwilliam, not me!* Angry tears gathered in her eyes until she had to blink them back. With a quick glance toward the dining room, a chilling realization struck: no one was coming after her. Georgiana wrapped her arms over her girlish bosom, shuddering in the suddenly cold corridor.

Moonbeams in the tall windows caught her attention. *I will ... take a constitutional in the rose garden! I always wanted to stroll there in the full moon. Despite what Fitzwilliam says, it is not improper at all.* Invigorated by the surge of defiance, she tossed her head and slipped out the door. The gravel poked her toes, triumphing over the slippers' thin soles. She shrugged off the pain. A chill breeze rattled the rose bushes. The canes swayed and whispered to each other.

"Oh!" A stray branch snapped back, tearing her wrist with a thorn. Her heart quickened, staring at the bloody trickle. She caught it with her tongue to avoid staining her sleeve, and inhaled deeply to calm herself.

At night, the garden smells like mama. Eyes closed, she drank in the fragrances surrounding her. *Why would*

Fitzwilliam deny me this! She stamped her foot, wincing when a small rock bruised her heel. "Ouch!" The pain fueled her outrage, and she had to flee.

Hobbling along the path, she wound through a wild tangle of thorny canes until the bushes obscured the windows' brightness. Each breath seared her knotted chest. After many shuddering gasps, the constriction eased, and she peeked at her environs. *Mama said leaving the roses a little wild gave them personality.* She stooped to rub her foot and collided with a cluster of full blossoms, their color indistinct in the silvery light. The heady fragrance filled her awareness. *Mama, I miss you so!* Silent tears cascaded. *You would not have been so mean to me tonight. Why did you leave me?* She sank to her knees and wept.

* * * * * * * *

From across the room, Darcy watched Caroline's flushed features and spiteful expression. His shoulders drooped, and he drew his hand down his face. Mrs. Cooperton followed his gaze and nodded. She took her leave and ambled toward Caroline.

"You are uncomfortable." Mrs. Cooperton installed herself beside her on the long, green settee. "This is not a fashionable London drawing room. Three days' ride makes us a world apart, no?"

Caroline huffed.

Bradley struck his opening chord. Edwards and Bingley joined in.

"I must say, that is an uncommonly pleasing rendition. Not the entertainment you are accustomed to in town, though."

"No, this is surely not London," Caroline muttered, staring at her brother through narrowed eyes.

"Nor will it ever be. We are a simple gathering of friends, celebrating the felicity among us." She adjusted the substantial ruby ring on her finger. "The good Lord knows we have shared enough tears together." She lowered her voice to just above a whisper. "Your cap is set at Mr. Darcy."

Caroline gasped and inched away, her cheeks crimson.

"Every young man of good fortune must be in want of a wife, eh?" She chortled while Caroline squirmed. "You appear dissatisfied by our familiarity and simple ways here in the wilds of the North. If you make an alliance with Darcy, this will be your lot."

"My brother has stayed with him at his townhouse. Mr. Darcy must spend much of the year there."

"Mr. Darcy, like his father before him, hates London. Many fashionable men stay months at a time in town, leaving their estates to their stewards. Mr. Darcy is a far better master."

Caroline's forehead puckered. She glanced from Mrs. Cooperton to Mr. Darcy and back again. "He seems easy enough in company *here*. If anything, too easy." She frowned and huffed. "My brother told me in *London*, Mr. Darcy is everything proper—"

"—and that he appreciates fine things and is keenly aware of what is fashionable."

"Precisely," Caroline sat straighter, "that is the very reason why my brother wished for us to meet. He believes Mr. Darcy and me very much alike."

"Of course, I understand now." She nodded slowly. "Your brother seeks to purchase an estate. You must be trying to leave your roots behind."

Caroline's blush deepened.

"I mean no offense, Miss Bingley. Many desire acceptance in the *ton*." Mrs. Cooperton patted her arm. "I am afraid Mr. Bingley misunderstands his friend."

"Excuse me?"

"Has Mr. Bingley not noted a difference, now you are here in Derbyshire?"

Caroline pursed her lips and cocked her head. "He said he was amazed at how amiable and easy Mr. Darcy seems, not at all the proper and fashion-conscious man he knew in town."

"Quite." She released a deep sigh and leaned into the soft cushions. "The Darcy of Derbyshire is the real man. In truth, he is shy in unfamiliar company. He lacks the natural ease others, like your brother, possess, finding it difficult to speak to strangers. Crowds are even worse. His consciousness of fashion and taste is merely his way to avoid giving offense. His father was the same. I suppose it is the mark of Darcy men. I tell you this only to save you the grief of misplaced affections."

"How dare you!" Caroline jumped up and flipped her skirt.

"Do not get your feathers ruffled, Miss Bingley." Mrs. Cooperton grasped her hand and pulled her to her seat. "I have been in society much longer than you. I dare say, I know the way of things." She shushed the forthcoming protests. "You are thinking about London drawing rooms, balls, and dinner parties. Mr. Darcy's heart is at Pemberley. He will expect much from the woman who becomes mistress of his estate."

Caroline smoothed her gown. "Certainly! He needs an accomplished lady at his side."

"What exactly are your accomplishments?"

Her narrow bosom puffed. "I draw and paint. I write with an elegant hand. I sing and play pianoforte, having studied under several of the best masters. My brother tells me I am the best dance partner he has ever had. My French and Italian are very good, although at needlework—"

"You certainly possess a remarkable education. However, do you understand the obligations of the mistress on an estate such as Pemberley?"

"Surely she must be his hostess, manage the menus, and servants—"

"Those are only a small part of her duties. I noticed you were distressed when Miss Darcy spoke of tending to tenants in need."

"I do my best to avoid *that* class of people." Caroline fidgeted and looked aside.

"I understand your brother is here to study estate management with Mr. Darcy. You should learn the role of mistress. After visiting Dunmore, come and stay with us at Allynden for a few days. I will be delighted to make those duties known to you."

Caroline swallowed hard, licking her lips. "I am flattered by your invitation; still, I must consult my brother."

"Consider him invited as well. Mr. Cooperton is quite taken with him. I heard him offer to help Mr. Bingley to find eligible properties."

"I ... I ... thank you. We will be pleased to visit you next week."

"Excellent! I shall go inform my husband."

·•·❧·•·❧·•·❧·•·❧·•·

Wickham stalked along the gravel path toward the stables. "Damn bloody bastard, trying to cheat me." He dodged the stable and skulked in the shadows to study the house.

An owl hooted in the distance, wings rustled, a tiny creature squawked. Wickham waited, hunkered in the bushes. When his thighs burned and his back cramped, he decided he had stayed long enough.

He quickly found the servants' door, his practiced movements nearly silent. *The dinner party will occupy them all.* He fished a chain from under his shirt and removed a heavy key. It clicked in the lock. The doorknob rattled, and he was inside.

Blackness veiled the constricted corridor, amplifying the thrum of his racing pulse. He paused and let his vision adjust to the tiny slivers of light sneaking under doorways and through minute cracks in paneling. Satisfied no one occupied the passageway, he scurried down the familiar path, letting his hand skim along the rough wall to guide him until he reached a pocket door. *Darcy will never know. I doubt he keeps count of the blunt[9] in his strongbox. Surely the key is still in the desk.* He grinned and tugged the door.

"Damn!" he muttered, cursing himself for speaking aloud. *He locked the bloody thing!*

He looked over his shoulder, though he could make out nothing in the darkness. *I am not going to leave here pauperized by that prig.[10]* Directed by touch alone, he picked his way up a narrow, steep stairway. The door handles all felt the same. He tried several before opening the one leading to Darcy's bedchamber.

He slipped in and found his target, a neat stack of bills in the top drawer. *Darcy will never notice this missing from the rag[11] he has here.* The bulk of the folded notes in his pocket brought on a smile that quickly became a sneer. *Why should he be in possession of all this?* He opened another drawer, his countenance softening a moment when he recognized the gold cuff links George Darcy once wore. *Losing these will drive him to distraction!* He licked his lips.

---

[9] Blunt: paper money
[10] Prig: Conceited, vain fellow
[11] Rag: paper money

Inside the nearly lightless servants' corridor, his blood tingled with the excitement of a horse race. Exhilaration rising, he counted his steps to find the entry to Georgiana's chamber. New possibilities raced through his mind. Ear pressed against the door panel, he listened for signs of an occupant and, hearing none, entered the pale blue sitting room.

He searched, finding nothing worth his while. Moments later, he opened the bedchamber. Anticipation left him breathless. *She does not enjoy her brother's tidy habits.* He laughed to himself. *Such an affront to the Darcy name!* Bitterness welled within. A sparkle caught his attention. Shoving aside a tangle of ribbon, he found a silver necklace set with a faceted blue stone. It joined the cufflinks. *Days may pass before she finds her pretty bauble gone. Too bad I will not be here to comfort her when she does.*

He peered through the window overlooking Lady Anne's rose garden. A small figure stood bathed in moonlight, her shoulders shuddering. A predatory fire burned in his belly. *Perhaps I may comfort her now.*

·•·க்ஷ·•·க்ஷ·•·க்ஷ·•·க்ஷ·•·க்ஷ·•·

Darcy leaned against the mantle and closed his eyes to listen to the soft refrains. *What would these last three years have been like without my friends?* He sighed, warmth washing over him. *Who else could extend me the grace of ignoring Georgiana's earlier behavior?*

Still standing at the pianoforte, Bingley asked, "Do you know any glees?"

"One or two, and, what is more, my friend here sings a passable baritone." Edwards raised his brows at Bradley who chuckled in surrender.

Soon they chose another piece, and the trio's rich voices resounded in a lively tune. A servant entered quietly and laid out a coffee service. Lackley helped himself and wandered over to Darcy.

"Excellent meal, Darcy." He lifted his cup in salute. "You have done so much to make us feel welcome since our arrival in the neighborhood."

"I am pleased you find yourself at ease among us." He paused a moment to look over at the singers. "Georgiana treasures your sister's friendship. Before you came, there was no one else her age nearby." Darcy pinched the bridge of his nose. "Her behavior tonight bewilders me."

"I do not always understand my own sister so well, either. Some moments, she seems a perfectly rational creature ..."

"And other moments, no amount of reason seems sufficient to persuade her?"

"Indeed!" Lackley guffawed, glancing at Bingley. "I wonder if your friend has the same impression of his sister."

"He does." Darcy noted Miss Bingley sitting alone. *That is a new expression for her ... I wonder, what is she plotting now? At least she is not staring at me.*

"Will our wives mystify us someday?"

"I cannot even begin to consider it!" Darcy peeked at the trio who brought their glee to a close.

Lackley glanced around the room. "I suppose time has come for the ladies to exhibit. Who do you fancy to begin?"

"Mrs. Cooperton is a superior musician, but will not be prevailed upon until the end of the evening, if at all. She argues her performing days are past, though she may give in after the other ladies have had their chance."

"Miss Bingley then?"

Darcy nodded and took a deep breath to fortify his resolve. Straightening his coat, he approached Miss Bingley and bowed. "Your brother speaks often of your skill on the pianoforte. Would you be so good as to play for us?" He offered his hand.

"I am honored, sir."

"Do play something lively for us, Caroline!" Bingley flipped through the sheet music.

"In due time, Charles." Caroline kept her mien neutral, though the tension in her jaw was evident.

The Coopertons shared an aggrieved look.

Darcy retreated to the fireplace.

Bradley joined him. "You honor me this night."

"I realize you do not seek such attention, but tonight it is fitting." Darcy's dark eyes crinkled.

"She plays a most intricate piece." Bradley jutted his chin toward the pianoforte.

"She plays to please her own tastes." Darcy laced his hands behind his neck and squeezed his temples with his elbows. "Perhaps she will yet heed her brother."

Edwards and Cooperton moved toward them, casting amused, furtive glimpses at Caroline.

"Enjoying the concerto?" Cooperton smirked.

Before Darcy managed a reply, Stephens rushed in. "Where is Mr. Wickham, sir? There is a problem in the stables with his horse that requires his immediate attention."

Darcy's face grew cold. His arms fell, leaden, to his sides. "I escorted him out after dinner and ordered the butler to bar him from the house."

"He did not leave the estate." Edwards smacked his fist into his palm.

"He must be found!" Darcy dashed out, Cooperton, Edwards and Bradley on his heels.

"You said he visited this afternoon. What did he want?" Bradley asked.

"Money. He inevitably comes with an open hand and an equally empty wallet." Darcy stood in the corridor, searching for signs of intrusion. "I caught him perusing my papers while he waited in the study. "

"What documents?" Edwards gripped Darcy's forearm hard.

"The only one I recognized from a distance was Father's old register book."

"What was in that ledger?" Cooperton leaned in close, worried lines etched across his brow.

"Records of accounts ..." Cold needles pricked along the back of Darcy's neck. "It had details of my sister's dowry!"

Cooperton grimaced. "You father purposed to keep the value a secret to protect her from—"

"—Wickham?" Fear seized his chest, constricting he thought his ribs would snap.. He bolted up the stairs, taking them two at a time.

Moments later, he flung open his sister's chamber door. "Georgiana!" Darcy's voice echoed off the walls. The moonlit rooms showed no signs of her. A sound from the window drew his attention. Throwing the curtains aside, he saw two figures in the shrubbery below. "The rose garden!"

* · ༂ঌ · · ༂ঌ · · ༂ঌ · · ༂ঌ · · ༂ঌ · ·

Georgiana bit her knuckle, trying to muffle her sob. *He does not care.* She rocked on her knees, the smell of loam triggering still more memories of her mother.

"Did he not send you to the nursery?"

Wickham's quiet voice made her jump. "George!"

"Should you not obey your brother's direction?" He helped her to her feet and brushed the dirt from her skirts.

"He was too cruel tonight!" Her chin quivered, and she blinked fiercely.

He wiped tears from her cheek with his thumb. "You know he cares for you, dearest."

"If he cares so much, why would he send me out? He treats me like a child!"

"He clearly does not see the young woman you have become." Fingertips traced her hairline. "A very lovely one." He smiled, his dark eyes wide.

"Tha … thank you." His lingering touch left her skin tingling. "No one has ever found me beautiful."

"They are fools." He bowed. "Will you walk?"

"Fitzwilliam does not allow me in the garden at night." She stole a glance at him. *He is so handsome. Everyone likes George. How many people like Fitzwilliam— always so serious and grim?*

"He has not the soul of a romantic."

"Yet you do."

He shrugged.

Shivers coursed down her back. "I am sorry, George, truly I am. My brother was so cruel to you. I cannot understand it."

He brushed a stray curl from her forehead, allowing his touch to dally on her cheek. "Of course not, dear one. What would a young lady like you know of the world's ways? Such is the stuff of men."

She laid her hand on his.

He tucked it in the crook of his elbow, guiding them further from the house.

"Why do you sigh?"

"My dearest," he stopped and looked at the moon, "there are things I should not say to you. I cannot … I must not."

"Tell me! Do not treat me like an infant! It is bad enough my brother does. I will not have that from you, as well." She tugged at his shoulder.

"A fire is in you, such a spark."

Georgiana felt her cheeks burn, her pulse throbbing. He pressed close enough for her to feel his warmth; dizziness threatened.

"What I would give to be the man who wins you. But, with neither home, nor prospects, your brother … no, such truths are not for delicate ears. You must forgive me."

"I do not understand." She clutched his hand, her breath coming in short pants.

"So innocent." He cupped her cheek, allowing his caress to drift down her neck.

"Explain it to me!"

"I have loved you for so long. Alas, that will have to be enough for me, for both of us, since I can never claim you as my own."

She stammered soft noises but no words formed.

"Shh, say nothing, my dear," he gently laid his finger on her mouth and kissed her forehead. "Unless …"

"Unless what, George? You have a plan?"

"Not a plan, sweet one. A hope, a dream, a possibility."

"Tell me."

"You can elope with me tonight."

"Elope?" She mouthed the word, her stomach clenching. Lightheaded, she staggered backward.

"It is the only way for us to be together. Your brother means to deny us our joy." He pulled her toward him. "Make me the happiest of men! Come away, tonight!"

She closed her eyes a moment, chewing her lip, wavering between possibilities. She planted her hands against his ribs. "George, I ... I cannot ..."

"Why?"

"Where would we go, how would we live? Surely my brother would not allow us to live here. You have no home—"

Crushing her to him, he whispered, "We will want for nothing. Your dowry is sufficient for us both." He kissed her violently.

Icy fear coursed through her limbs. She struggled in his unrelenting grasp. "No, no, stop!"

"What is wrong, my love?" He clutched her to his chest.

"Stop it, George! Let me go!" She fought to wrench herself from his embrace, kicking his shins and pounding his arms.

"My fiery little woman, you will be mine tonight!" Wrestling her under control, he smashed his lips to hers.

She screamed.

"Wickham!" Darcy bellowed, followed by many pounding footfalls.

Georgiana looked over Wickham's shoulder. Her panicked brother pounded toward her, two burly footmen at his sides. Her knees buckled.

A moment later, Darcy wrenched her from his grasp. Stephens and Davis immediately restrained Wickham's arms.

"Unhand me!" Wickham thrashed against the footmen.

Cooperton roared and hurled his fist into Wickham's ribs. "That is for the maids you ruined." Shaking his hand out, he muttered, "Been too long in coming!"

Wickham staggered, coughing and sputtering.

"Georgiana?" Darcy pried her off his coat, vying for a glimpse of her face. "What did he do to you?"

"She is compromised, Darcy." Wickham laughed hoarsely. "We must marry."

Georgiana inhaled sharply, all color drained from her face. "No, that is not what happened." Her strained whisper was lost in the night air.

"I have witnessed no compromise," Edwards snarled in Wickham's ear.

"Nor I." Bradley flanked Darcy.

Cooperton rubbed his balled fist in his other hand. "Without witnesses, there is no compromise. The young lady and her brother merely strolled in the gardens in the moonlight and came across you trespassing. Or have you forgotten that you were directed to leave here?"

Davis and Stephens mumbled something between themselves. Davis jerked Wickham's wrists together behind his back while Stephens searched his pockets. Moments later Stephens produced a wad of bank notes, the cuff links, and necklace.

"Beggin' your pardon, sirs." Stephens held out his findings. "He be a filching cover[12] seekin' to impose upon Miss Darcy."

"From the looks of it, he's took enough to get hisself hanged." Davis twisted Wickham's shoulders further.

"I kissed her! She must marry me!"

"No compromise occurred." Edwards crossed his arms and glared.

"He kissed me!" She sobbed into Darcy's coat. "I told him to stop and pushed him away. He would not …"

"Do not fear." He wrapped his arms tightly around her. "He will trouble you no further."

"But he said … he called me … he wanted to …"

Darcy pulled her into his shoulder, silencing her.

"Bingley and his sister!" Wickham winced, fighting Davis's hold. "She will not hesitate to speak of it. Such a piece of gossip will be too much for her to resist, unless, of course, you pay her off, perhaps by marrying her!"

"They know nothing." Edwards shoved Wickham backward one step, then another.

Wickham's feet slid out from beneath him, only the footmen's hold prevented him from an ignoble fall into the dirt.

"I will return to the manor and inform them Miss Darcy is suddenly unwell and company is not safe for

---

[12] Filching cover: male thief

her right now." Deep worry lines etched Bradley's face. "Lackley invited the Bingleys to visit. I am sure he will be willing to take them to Dunmore tonight."

Cooperton joined them. "If you are agreeable, I will ask my wife to stay at Pemberley. A girl needs a mothering soul in moments like this."

"Do it."

They hurried off.

"Oh, Fitzwilliam, I am so sorry." Georgiana blinked up at him, trembling in his embrace.

"Tomorrow is soon enough for talk. Tonight, I insist you allow Mrs. Cooperton to stay with you. She was a dear friend to our mother, and she will be a friend to you."

"No! What will she think of me?" She hid her face in his lapels.

"Georgiana!" His tone became sharp. "You desire to be treated as an adult, so now, you must act like one!"

She gasped, startled at his uncharacteristic firmness. Her chin quivered.

More softly, he asked, "Have you done wrong tonight?"

"Yes." Her voice broke. She could not meet his eyes.

"Do you want to be forgiven?"

"More than anything else!" She sniffled into her hands, hiding her face in shame. "You all must hate me now!"

"No one hates you." He stroked her hair. "But you must make things right."

"How?" The bitter taste of panic coated her tongue.

He grasped her shoulders and shook her lightly. "Bradley admonishes us to take responsibility for what we have done, to confess our wrongs, and make restitution for them then commit to do different in the future. Is that not the true nature of repentance?" He held her at arm's length to look into her eyes. "Do it now. Go to those you wronged and make it right. They will be quick to forgive."

"Must I?" The thought tore at her pride. She fought not to run from his demands.

"How else can you see them again? Would you rather live always wondering if they continue to hold your foolishness against you?"

She winced at the painful word. "Surely they are angry. What if they do not forgive me?"

"I have no doubt they will. They have been our friends for too long not to."

They heard footsteps and recognized the Coopertons approaching. Before Georgiana uttered a word, Mrs. Cooperton embraced her. "My dear child! Thank heavens you are well!"

"I am so sorry." She cried into Mrs. Cooperton's ample breast.

"I know. We will talk about all this difficult business in the morning. Come, all will be well." She led Georgiana away.

5 A MAN REAPS WHAT HE SOWS

Wickham shouted and demanded release, but his cries fell on deaf ears. Darcy and Cooperton turned their backs and returned to the house, only increasing his rage. He snarled out a storm of expletives at the footmen who, led by Edwards, manhandled him to Bradley's old cottage and bound him to a chair in the dining room. Throat raw, he panted, glaring at his captors. The ropes cut into his arms. He squirmed, trying to avoid the loose straw from the wicker seat poking into his thigh. His eyes followed Edwards out of the room, wondering what new indignity would be heaped upon him.

Edwards returned a few moments later, bearing a nearly full magnum of port and two glasses. He filled the goblets and released the bindings constricting

Wickham's left hand. "Behave yourself, or these men will not hesitate to act."

The footmen grunted.

"Unlike some here," Wickham craned his neck to glower at Darcy's men, "*you* are a truly civilized man." He flexed and stretched his hand before he took the glass. "Is all this really necessary?" He pointed his chin at the ropes and tugged against them.

Edwards sipped his wine.

Wickham stifled the angry retort that danced on his tongue and, with a deceptively mild shrug, swallowed his words with a mouthful of wine. "You brought out the fine stuff, sir. What is this, the last pleasures of a condemned man?" He laughed, a bitter note lingering in the aftertaste.

"I gave it to Bradley last year. He has yet to move all his things to the parsonage."

"Clearly, the old finger post[13] never appreciated it. I, on the other hand, am always ready to savor a fine vintage." Wickham laughed and drew another mouthful.

Edwards leaned in, knuckles under his chin. "You make jokes when you ought to be considering the peril you face."

"What peril?" Wickham tossed back the remaining claret and landed the crystal heavily. "Darcy would not dare prosecute me." He rolled his eyes, sniffing.

---

[13] Finger post: a parson, so called because he points the way to others but does not go there himself

"Are you so sure?" Edwards replenished his drink. "You stole his property—"

"A few trinkets—nothing he cares for." Wickham flicked his fingers. "He would not even have noticed—"

"—had you not tried to impose upon Miss Darcy."

"Ah, sweet Georgiana." Raising his goblet, Wickham swirled it, admiring the contents and drank again.

"The girl or her dowry?"

A wry smile pulled at Wickham's cheeks, his eyebrows arched suggestively.

Edwards's features took on a sharpness that left Wickham squirming. "Were you not studying—"

"Academics do not appeal to me. One needs a dour temperament, like Darcy's, to support the tedium. He found endless hours of study fascinating." He emptied his port again, noticing the ropes seemed to chafe less now. "I found it a bore. I would much rather visit an academician[14] than become one." His laugh ended with a small hiccup.

Edwards grunted. "So how did you employ yourself? Your father hoped—"

Wickham slammed the table.

The footmen jumped and turned to Edwards. A small motion of his hand halted them.

"He was a fool, dying with nothing to show for his existence. Darcy's father favored me, not his stiff-

---

[14] Academician: prostitute at a brothel or a scholar at an academy

backed son. 'e said I would 'ave a gentleman's life."
Wickham reached for his refilled chalice.

"You spent Darcy's legacy on the devil's dance[15] and
lightskirts![16] Did one of them tip you the token?[17]"

Wickham choked on his port, coughing a few drops
onto the tablecloth.

"Your benefactor would be disappointed. He did
not hope for you to be a gentleman of three outs.[18] Are
you deep enough in dun territory[19] to be fearin' a clap
on the shoulder?[20]" Edwards frowned, rubbing his
palms together. "What town's merchants are you
running from? Tell me, or shall I guess?"

Wickham fingered his glass, nearly tipping it. "Oops!
Should not let that go to waste!" He gulped the
remnants of the claret.

Edwards studied him. "You favor your mother."

"You knew her?" Wickham blinked hard several
times, trying to focus.

"I did. Shall I tell you of her?"

"That is as fair a way as any to pass the hours."
Wickham's head lolled against the chair.

Propping his boots on the table, Edwards spoke of
Lavinia Wickham, who survived just five years after
giving birth to her son. She pampered her only child,

---

[15] Devil's dance: gambling
[16] Lightskirts: prostitutes
[17] Tip the token: to give a venereal disease
[18] Gentleman of three outs: without wits, without money and without manners
[19] Dun territory: debt
[20] Clap on the shoulder: arrest for debt

spoiling him from the earliest days. Edwards reminded him of her peculiar, lisping voice, her odd grey eyes, and her fondness for smoked kippers in the evenings. Three glasses of port later, Edwards finished his narrative.

Wickham worked his tongue against the roof of his mouth and pulled at his bonds, momentarily forgetting why he had been restrained. "You knew … Mama?"

"I did."

Wickham held up his empty glass.

Edwards replenished the ruby liquid. "So how long did you ride to get here? I recall you were quite the horseman."

"Bettah dan Dahcy," he rolled his head along the wooden chair slats. "T'was a day and an hour on horseback."

"Had you a pleasant journey?"

"Foolz! Dey thinks themse'ves clevah wit' a writ o' debt![21] Child's play ta keep 'way fom 'em!" He laughed, knocking over his wine. The few remaining drops slid onto the ivory cloth, staining it crimson. "T'was da gamahrs dat kept me r-runnin'! I 'spose I'll be r-runnin' ag'in soon." His head bobbed while his left hand played ineffectively at the knots.

"I think not." Edwards slid his feet down, boots echoing against the floor.

Wickham clutched the table, squinting and blinking, trying to bring the double images of Edwards into one.

---

[21] Writ for debt: arrest warrant for debt

"Donna' be thweatenin' me now. You willna' go tellin' da magistwate no mo' dan Dahcy." He struggled to sit in his chair without losing his balance.

"Mr. Wickham," Edwards laced his fingers and rubbed his palms together, "I am the magistrate."

·•• 🙨🙦 ·•· 🙨🙦 ·•· 🙨🙦 ·•· 🙨🙦 ·•· 🙨🙦 •·

Georgiana's distress and Wickham's smug satisfaction, both so out of place amidst Lady Anne's roses, rattled the depths of Bradley's soul. Every part of him rebelled against standing rationally, alternately yearning to throttle Wickham and to shake Georgiana.

Darcy would tell me to calm myself. Bradley rapidly shuffled down the path, arms clutched to his belly. *He does not know.* He paused, staring at the moonlight, finding no comfort in its cool radiance. Gulping air, he willed his racing heart to slow against the growing ache in his chest. *She is safe. Nothing else matters.* He hurried on, desperate to vent the anxious, scorching energy roiling in his guts. *Did she not grasp the danger?* He shook his head. *She had not the means.* Breathless, he stopped, still panting hard. *The cur did not ruin her, but there was no doubt as to his intentions ... How can this be happening all over again?*

A few minutes later, a single candle lit the front of the church. Bradley paced in the flickering glow, his footsteps ringing in the otherwise empty building. He abandoned vain attempts to calm his violent emotions as waves of tortured memories flooded over him.

"How could You?" he shouted, shaking a fist at the ceiling. "Why are You forcing me to relive it?" He slammed his palm against the heavy wood of a nearby pew. "Was taking my Emily from me not sufficient? Now You allow Georgiana to fall prey …" His voice broke, and he fell to his knees.

"Was it not enough You took her parents?" He clambered to his feet. "Were You not watching over her? You failed her! Is Your arm too short to save? If You are so worthy, how could You fail me?"

Pounding footfalls resonated against the stone walls. He turned to stalk toward the other wall, pausing at the unadorned wooden bookstand that held his heavily worn bible. With a scornful snort, he threw the book open. The pages parted to a well-worn place. Bradley did not need to read the tear-stained words to know what they said. A crushing weight descended. He crumpled to the floor. Face in his hands, ragged sobs tore from his soul. He remembered …

His friend and mentor, David Allen, stood beside him as Bradley stared at the fresh grave, the evening chill cutting sharply through the air.

"He already demanded her mother from me at Emily's birth," he said, his breaths coming in shallow, searing pants.

"John, you are grieving …"

"What can you tell me of grief? You will go home to your wife and daughters! My cottage is empty!" He hid his face in his hands.

"His ways are not like ours. You must remember that. They are better than ours—"

His head snapped up. "Better? My only daughter was seduced and made with child! Are those His ways? Now she has died in her confinement, and you claim this is superior? I cannot accept ..." He stalked to the gate. The iron hinges sang mournfully. Clutching the cold metal, he called over his shoulder, "Tell me this improves upon what I wanted? How do I have faith in a God who ..." he pointed toward the grave, his words threatening to suffocate him. "You expect me to still believe?" His fury spent, Bradley's voice was nearly lost to the wind.

Allen rushed to him and guided them to a bench. They sat in silence until the damp chill penetrated their coats. The piercing gusts cut their faces and warned of nightfall's impending descent. "I have no easy answers for you. In fact, I know very little." He frowned, averting his gaze. "Do you believe Emily and her mother are resting in the bosom of our Savior?"

Bradley chewed his lip, and squirmed against the cold stone. He drummed his fingers and scrunched his face, exhaling heavily. "Yes. That knowledge alone keeps me from going mad."

"Does not the Apostle Paul write: 'To live is good, but to die and join our heavenly Father is far better?' Perhaps we hold on too tightly to this life. She now feels neither sorrow nor suffering and no longer battles with those who condemned her. He condemns her not."

Tears coursed down Bradley's face.

"He does not take lightly the deaths of His saints." Allen rubbed his chin. "I cannot fathom why this happened. Through it all, I have only one thing of which I am sure, and it must be enough."

"What is that?"

"God is good. All I see, all I know, convinces me of it."

Bradley grumbled through clenched jaws.

"Either He is always good, or He is not. Our understanding has no bearing on His nature. If His ways and His thoughts are not as ours, is it any surprise we do not comprehend? You must choose. Is He good, and these things are beyond our ken? Or, should we believe nothing the Holy Scripture tells us?"

Bradley muttered under his breath, weighing the two unpalatable options.

Allen brushed silver hair out of his eyes. "Decide, John. Turn away from Him now. Find comfort where you can— in honest work, in food and drink, in the arms of a warm woman, or embrace faith and believe, trusting His grace will be sufficient, whether you grasp His ways or not. Choose!"

The demand resounded in Bradley's ears, burning into his mind. "How can you ask that of me?" He groaned into his hands, rocking in time to his torn breaths.

"If not now, when?"

Bradley stomped away.

Bradley's ragged sobs slowly subsided. He recalled the night that he made his choice, alone in his cottage, those he loved gone. He wiped his face on his sleeve and stared at the ceiling. "None of this makes sense to me, Lord, but I am certain of Your goodness. I must not lose myself in the past. This is a new day." Heaving himself up, he smiled crookedly.

He dusted off his knees and resettled his glasses. "Now I have finished my mad ranting—Lord, you are indeed patient—it is time for me to seek Your wisdom." He shuffled to his old Bible, reading for a few moments. With a renewed sense of purpose and strength coursing through him, Bradley returned to the altar and began his prayers in earnest.

· • *&~&* · • *&~&* · • *&~&* · • *&~&* · • *&~&* · •

The house eerily quiet, Darcy sat bleary-eyed in his study. He stared into the flickering fireplace, hoping to clear the echoes of Miss Bingley's shrill voice from his memory. *Is Georgiana thought to be contagious? Has the doctor been sent for! Fetch my maid to pack!* He laughed under his breath, Mrs. Reynolds's huff and eye roll flashing in his mind.

Shortly thereafter, he wrote a letter to Richard and dispatched a rider. That done, he sat at his desk, searching for useful employment, or, in the absence of that, company. Cooperton had gone to his estate and would not return for hours yet. Mrs. Cooperton attended Georgiana upstairs. Edwards detained Wickham, and Bradley was nowhere to be found.

Darcy pushed himself up and paced around the room, desperate to escape the smothering sense of hopelessness. *Father, you gave Wickham whatever he asked. Yet, you said "no" to me easily enough. Were you unaware of the ... man ... you were creating?* "I always resented you for that," Darcy muttered, worrying the marble paperweight. Acid heat scorched his cheeks as he waited to hear his father's reprimand. The voice never came, and aching loneliness settled into his belly like soured milk. "Father, what do I do now?"

Darcy meandered to the bookcase. His fingertips traced the bindings of several ornate tomes. *You warned me not to violate the privacy of your journals.* The frayed spine snagged his fingertip when he removed the volume. *I need your voice, Father. I need you.* The journal tight under his arm, he settled into the chair by the fire.

Forgive me for this. The tooled leather conjured long forgotten memories— his father's face, his voice, even his scent— until Darcy felt his presence in the room.

He opened the cover, trying to ignore its creaking complaints. His father's familiar script drew him in. George Darcy's voice spoke the words he read. Though the first entry simply told of spring plantings, new farming methods and a minor tenant dispute, the ache in Darcy's chest eased. He raked his hair and slumped. The fire popped; he took up the poker, stirred the flames and added a log.

Anticipating the next passage, he returned to his seat. Differences in the handwriting signaled a distinct change in the writer's mood.

My dearest Anne is angry with me once again. In truth, I cannot blame her. Fitzwilliam went to her, upset.

Darcy heard his father's sigh. His mother had often intervened between them, soothing their tensions and forging the bond that would eventually tie them so strongly.

My son came to me asking for favors— this time, a horse. I should not have given it to him, but I am unable to deny the boy. I presented him the gelding.

Anne tells me I do him no favors by giving him everything he asks for and fears he will never make anything of himself because of my indulgence with him.

She looks at me with those eyes and my heart breaks. What have I done?

Darcy paused, brows knotted. *What? I did not ask him for the stallion he gave me on my birthday. George was so jealous. Not a month later …* Icy chills dripped down his face and into his limbs. His hands shaking, he flipped through the pages and read the line over and over—*my son.*

The color drained from his cheeks, his guts twisting into tangles. There, in his father's own script: George Wickham was his son. The journal fell forgotten as Darcy's world collapsed in on him, crushing the breath from his chest.

Late in the night, four of Edwards's men relieved Davis and Steven. Wickham immediately recognized they were of a different cut. When one addressed him as "Major Edwards" he understood. Dread crept over him until sometime in the early morning when he finally surrendered to fitful sleep.

Hours later, he cracked open his eyes. Two men sat beside him, playing chess in the pale light of dawn. He screwed his lids shut, blocking the burning brightness. The warm scent of coffee drifted up, leaving him vaguely nauseated.

"Sanderson, Elmer." Edwards's boots clomped too loudly.

"Everything you asked for is in the kitchen. Me an' Sanderson brung it," Elmer said, focused on the game board.

"And there's coffee a'plenty." Sanderson laughed, winking.

Moments later, Edwards returned with a steaming mug and a plate. "When did you relieve the others?" He sat across from Wickham.

"Sanderson and me took o'er 'bout two hours ago, Major." Elmer looked up from the chessboard.

"Once he saw he could not talk hisself loose, he shut up and fell asleep. Been right nice company since!" Sanderson shoved his elbow into Elmer's ribs, grinning.

After his last bite, Edwards pushed his plate aside. Wickham stirred, drawing up his head with a groan. He blinked painfully in the morning light, skull throbbing and eyes sandy.

"Quite a headache you are nursing, I imagine." Edwards drained his coffee.

"Ugh!" Wickham grunted, smacking his lips.

"Food?"

He nodded and grimaced, fighting to swallow the tang of vomit.

"Elmer, bring our guest something to eat. Promise to behave, and Sanderson will untie you so you can feed yourself."

Wickham's head bobbed unsteadily. Sanderson untied his hand and seated himself on Wickham's left. Elmer dropped a plate and landed a cup beside it. Wickham brought the mug to his mouth and sneered at the biting black brew.

"You do not prefer coffee?"

"Bitter, uncivilized stuff," Wickham muttered. He abandoned the beverage and took a bite of bread to mask the flavor.

Elmer and Sanderson returned to their chess while Edwards watched. At length, Sanderson tipped his king.

"Excellent game, Elmer." Edwards clapped his shoulder. "Not the green batman I used to best in just four moves."

"Been a long day since you could do that!" Elmer laughed and reset the board. "There's a pint ya' owe me." He winked at Sanderson.

"Not if I take your king this time!"

Wickham grumbled, drawing his hand over his face and through his oily hair. "Enough of this game,

Edwards. Untie me and let me on my way," he rasped, his tongue thick against the cotton in his mouth.

"Excuse me?" Edwards's eyebrow lifted high.

"I will remove myself from Pemberley, and all may return as it was." He banged the table hard enough to rattle the chess pieces.

"I cannot do it."

"Why the blazes not!" He waved violently, lunging toward Edwards. His stomach lurched, threatening to dispel its contents.

Sanderson grabbed Wickham's arm.

"Call off your dog, Edwards!"

"Carry on."

Wickham resisted while Sanderson bound his hand. "I have had my fill of this. Darcy has his baubles, no harm done. Surely he is as anxious for my absence as I am to take my leave."

"You forget," Edwards rested his chin on his fist, "you are a common thief."

"You make a crime out of nothing at all! Besides, Darcy will never press charges."

"Darcy's wishes are irrelevant. The law of the land prosecutes. I promised to uphold it when I took the office of magistrate."

"I have learned my lesson. I will not bother Darcy again." Wickham struggled against the ropes, hoping he would not cast up his accounts.[22]

---

[22] Cast up one's accounts: vomit

"What you did last night, Mr. Wickham, is a hanging offense. What is more, I suspect a writ of debt has been issued for you in Manchester. It will do nothing to help your case. Your best expectation is prison or transportation."

"Darcy! He will speak on my behalf, his father—"

"I doubt it. Have you forgotten what you tried to do to his sister?"

Fear snaked down Wickham's spine, and his face blanched.

"I suppose you are not a man of prayer. This may be an excellent time to change, though, since I am not disposed to mercy right now. Justice seems more appealing."

* · ᕦᕤ · * · ᕦᕤ · * · ᕦᕤ · * · ᕦᕤ · * · ᕦᕤ · *

After the initial shock and revulsion wore off, Darcy poured over his father's journals, far into the night until the dawn peeked through the windows.

Wickham was his son. He ran his fingertip along the inked page. *I was theirs.*

> *Bradley insists I must forgive myself, but how? Every time I see the hurt in Anne's eyes, I hate myself all over again. I look at the boy and find a younger version of myself.*
>
> *Our son has his mother's eyes.*
>
> *Anne assures me of her forgiveness. She says her hurt is no longer for what I did, but for what I am doing now.*

I have already done so much wrong by my son. How am I to deny him the little I have left to give?

I hope our boy will understand someday. I am proud of the man he is becoming. That is surely his mother's influence.

Bradley warns me that a good father disciplines the son whom he loves. I suppose he is right. My friend forces me to accept the sad truth. I do not love the boy. I feel guilt, and it is enough to keep me jumping at his every whim.

The fact brings me no pride.

I do not love the boy … Darcy set the journal aside and threw his arm over his face. "All these years, I believed he loved George Wickham better than me. But he never did … oh, Father!" A bitter weight slipped from his shoulders.

He stood and stretched, reveling in the lightness he felt. "No wonder you lectured me to keep myself under good regulation when I left home!" A blanket of weariness descended. "I must speak to Bradley, but first, sleep. What a legacy you have given me, Father!"

He trudged upstairs to his room and fell into bed, stopping only to pull off his boots and cravat.

6 YOUR SIN WILL FIND YOU OUT

Georgiana screwed her eyes shut against the beams of morning sunlight pouring into her windows. She tugged the blanket over her head and shoved her pillow over her ears in a vain attempt to block the voices still resonating in her mind. *What I would give to be the man who wins you ... I have loved you for so long ... elope tonight ... She is compromised ... You do not comprehend the danger ...* "Argh!" She threw the pillow aside and fought her way free from the counterpane.

She sat up and gulped several deep breaths, willing her racing thoughts to cease. "I am sure it was all a simple misunderstanding." Bedclothes tangled in her feet, and she nearly fell. Catching herself on the bedpost, she shoved the linens away and reached for her dressing gown. The wool bristled against the back of her neck, adding to her ill humor.

She dropped into her favorite overstuffed chair, landing in a most unladylike posture. *They misconstrued everything. George was not trying to force me to elope, merely passionate in his declarations. It was my fault; I overreacted. Had I not screamed, all would be well. I might even be engaged!* She rubbed her hands along her forearms. *Fitzwilliam misjudged everything. He is always so ready to condemn George. The Coopertons and Mr. Bradley, too. I am sure we can come to a resolution over breakfast. They will realize all this to-do is but "Much Ado about Nothing."* She laughed, smiling to herself.

Not long afterwards, she hurried downstairs, full of hopes for a quick resolution. Muffled voices in conversation encouraged her optimism, only to have it dashed when she found Mr. and Mrs. Cooperton alone in the dining room.

Swallowing her disappointment, she muttered, "Good morning." Little seemed appetizing as she served her plate from the sideboard. Unable to contain a heavy sigh, she joined the Coopertons at the table, leaving a few empty seats between herself and her guests.

The tiny noises of eating filled the room, growing louder in the absence of dialog.

Cooperton cleared his throat. "The weather has certainly taken a turn for the better. What a delightful break in the rain."

"As much as my flower garden loves the rains, I grow tired of all the grey clouds and gloom. Do you not, Miss Darcy?" Mrs. Cooperton's pointed expression left Georgiana fidgeting.

"Yes. I find a sunny morning much more agreeable than a dreary one." Georgiana glanced over her shoulder. "Is my brother about, Mr. Cooperton?"

"Not yet. I believe he retired only a little while ago." Cooperton pushed a kipper onto a bit of bread and popped it in his mouth.

Crestfallen, she huffed and stared at her plate. "He is usually an early riser."

"Last night was quite trying." Mrs. Cooperton buttered her muffin. "I am sure he will see you this afternoon after he has had opportunity to refresh himself."

"I am sure you are correct." Georgiana straightened her spine against her disappointment and lifted her teacup. "I simply anticipated resolving this misunderstanding—" A sharp sniff interrupted her.

"Ladies, excuse me." Cooperton rose. "I have correspondence to attend." He scowled at Georgiana.

Indignation flamed her cheeks as she watched his quick exit. A curt remark formed on her lips; however, Mrs. Cooperton flashed a dark look, and she thought better of it. For a long time, they ate in silence.

Georgiana sensed Mrs. Cooperton's severe gaze and squirmed under the scrutiny. She avoided eye contact, hoping to evade any further discussion. Finished eating, she shoved her plate aside and hurried to leave.

"Georgiana—"

She grumbled under her breath.

"—would you please join me in the blue sitting room, near my chambers? We need to talk, and this is not the place for the conversation we must have."

Georgiana searched her mind for excuses, stammering in the meantime. Her ploy fell short when Mrs. Cooperton grasped her elbow and led her upstairs. She tried to pull away but found it impossible to do so without causing a scene. In the sitting room, she chose a seat as far from Mrs. Cooperton as was possible.

"I was blessed with five children, two of them daughters." Mrs. Cooperton walked to the window, her back to Georgiana whose prickling skin left her twitching on the settee. "You remind me of my girls."

Georgiana tossed her head scornfully, wondering how long she would prattle on.

"All girls go through a period where they are neither a little girl nor a grown-up woman. It is a trying time: a stage of chafing under rules that no longer seem to fit, of romantic notions—and foolish deeds."

The words stung so sharply Georgiana gasped.

"Last night I told you I did not believe you understood the degree of jeopardy in which you placed yourself. Now I am certain of it."

Georgiana's brow wrinkled. "I disobeyed my brother. I went into the garden at night instead of the nursery. I allowed George to speak to me without a chaperone. When he spoke of eloping, I considered it, just for a moment. I know it improper, but *so* romantic. He declared he loved me. Everyone is at sixes and sevens over nothing—"

"Enough!" Mrs. Cooperton's hands slashed the air as she rounded on Georgiana. "You know naught of love. You ignore the direction of a loving brother and put yourself in the power of a man who never loved anyone save himself!"

"No! Perhaps George was wrong, yet what else may be expected when everyone treats him unfairly ..."

"Do not bemoan his hardships in my presence again." Her visage darkened, her voice hard. "You will not continue referring to Mr. Wickham in so familiar a manner. It is most inappropriate. Do you wish people to consider you a ladybird[23] or accuse your brother of raising one? "

Georgiana shook her head, wide-eyed. "How can you say—"

"What do you consider are Mr. Wickham's misfortunes?"

Georgiana jumped to her feet unable to contain the surging, violent energy. "Father promised him the Kympton living, but Fitzwilliam gave it to Mr. Bradley."

"Your father wanted Mr. Bradley to have the living first, perhaps taking Mr. Wickham as a curate to train him up. He never intended for Mr. Wickham to have it instead of Mr. Bradley. Besides, Mr. Wickham is not fit for the church."

Georgiana crossed her arms tightly over her chest. "That is not fair! Who are you to cast judgment? Why

---

[23] Ladybird: a woman of easy virtue who trades her favors for money or gifts

do you condemn Geo—I mean Mr. Wickham's character? He is very kind to me—"

"His kindness is not what you think. Sit down." She rang for her maid. "Lilly, bring them in."

"Yes, ma'am." Lilly curtsied.

A moment later, two young women arrived at the door. Although clean and neat, their drab dresses made their positions in service clear. "Miss Darcy, Millie and Patty."

The girls dipped awkwardly.

"Take a seat. You must not share this conversation with anyone, ever." She reached into her purse, withdrew several coins, and pressed them into their palms.

They gaped at the glittering shillings.

"We promise, ma'am," Millie whispered, tucking the money into her pocket.

Mrs. Cooperton nodded curtly. "I need you to acquaint Miss Darcy with the character of Mr. George Wickham."

The immediate change in the maids' countenances startled Georgiana.

"I insist you speak openly in this matter. Nothing you say in this room will be held against you."

"Beggin' your pardon, miss," Patty snuck a quick glimpse at Millie, " 'e's not fit to speak of in polite company."

"No?" Georgiana sat bolt upright.

"No, mum." Millie shook her head slowly.

" 'e is the worst sort." Patty leaned forward against her thighs. " 'e says 'e is a gentleman, and then leaves a girl high in the belly."

Georgiana sprang to her feet, glaring at the maid. "How dare you! I have heard enough—"

"She says these things because they are true. Now sit and listen." Mrs. Cooperton took her by the wrist.

She ripped her arm away and wrapped it around her waist, glowering.

"Go on, Patty."

"Beggin' your pardon ma'am, that rake, 'e took to 'anging about me sister two years ago. 'e talked all pretty and made 'er believe they would marry. When she told 'im she sprained 'er ankle,[24] 'e laughed and left, nary speaking to 'er ag'in." Patty balled the fabric of her skirts in her fists, her fair skin flushed. "Me father sent 'er to Scotland. I will never see 'er ag'in."

"No! He said —"

"—'e loved you, miss?" Patty glanced at Mrs. Cooperton. " 'e done told my sister too, but 'e loves nothing 'cept gettin' his chimney swept out![25]"

Georgiana blushed at the indelicate language, from a girl no less! She tucked her chin and focused on the suddenly fascinating stitchery of her bodice.

"It is true, Miss Darcy," Millie whispered. She shrank at Georgiana's scowl. "It were not jes' her he done bagged. My sister an' me looked jes alike, an' he

---

[24] Sprained her ankle: became pregnant
[25] Getting his chimney swept out: sexual intimacy with a woman

thought her a pretty bit o' muslin. He couldna tell us apart and sometimes—"

"Enough! I do not want to—" Georgiana turned aside.

"I care not what you want to hear. Turn around, now." Mrs. Cooperton pushed her shoulder.

Pouting, she complied.

"Millie, continue."

"He left 'er belly full." Millie sniffled and swallowed hard. "She died trying to birth his stall whimper.[26] He killed my sister sure as if he slit her throat." She swiped her sleeve across her eyes.

Mrs. Cooperton passed Millie a handkerchief and rang for Lilly. "Take them to the kitchen and given them tea and biscuits."

"Yes, ma'am." Lilly ushered them out.

"What do you think of your 'beau' now?" Mrs. Cooperton's foot tapped, the soft sound piercing the room's chill silence.

They are lying! Georgiana strode to the window, her mind whirling. She remembered his words in the garden, his tender profession of love and suggestion— or was it a demand—to elope. His countenance brightened when he spoke ... of her dowry. *Those girls are without a portion ... he said he loved them ... but wanted to marry me.* She gasped. *It was the money!* "How could he do those things with other girls? He told he loved me for so long ..." She wept into her hands. "He lied to me."

---

[26]Stall whimper: illegitimate child

"Your father kept your worth a mystery to protect you from men like Wickham." Mrs. Cooperton drew Georgiana into her arms.

"Fitzwilliam knew. Is that why he did not give George ... Mr. Wickham the living?"

"Yes. Your brother has known him a long time and tried to help him but, Mr. Wickham is a man without principles." She stroked Georgiana's hair softly.

"Surely Father saw it, too. Why did he love Mr. Wickham so much?"

"I cannot say, my dear. I never understood."

· • ᴖ⚬ᴗᴖ · • · ᴖ⚬ᴗᴖ · • · ᴖ⚬ᴗᴖ · • · ᴖ⚬ᴗᴖ · • · ᴖ⚬ᴗᴖ • ·

Later in the afternoon, refreshed and more alert, Darcy retreated to the sanctuary of his study. He massaged his temples, hoping answers would come. *Where do I begin?* A meek knock broke his reverie. "Come in."

Georgiana peeked in.

He noticed Mrs. Cooperton over her shoulder. Rising, he beckoned her in.

"Go on." Mrs. Cooperton gently shoved her through the door and closed it.

"I am a fool!" Georgiana threw herself at him so hard he stepped back to catch his balance. "I accused you of treating Mr. Wickham unfairly, yet all along it was you being used unkindly!" Darcy tried to answer, but she gripped his wrist to silence him. "No, please, let me speak. I must!"

"I will listen." He led her to a chair and encouraged her to sit.

"I was wrong to take Mr. Wickham's word over yours. You cared for me and protected me, all the more after Father died. I should not have listened to him criticize you, but in my vanity, I enjoyed his flattery. Then I disgraced you in front of our friends. I even insulted Mr. Bradley." Rivulets of tears dripped over her cheeks and onto her dress. "You were right to dismiss me from your company."

Darcy hunkered down beside her.

"I defied you and walked outside. What a romantic notion!" She rubbed her handkerchief over her cheeks and wadded it into her hand. "Mrs. Cooperton brought two of her maids ..." Her voice quivered. "Mr. Wickham dallied with their sisters and ruined them both. One died in childbirth. The other will spend her life banished to Scotland. How easily it might have been me!"

He gathered her into his arms as much for his comfort as for hers.

"Please, forgive me!"

"I do." His embrace tightened around her. "I regret you had to know George Wickham's true nature ... but I am so relieved you understand now." He brushed a loose curl out of her face. "I have written for Cousin Richard to come. I will ask him to take you to Aunt Matlock. She will help you—"

"Please do not send me away, I promise—"

"You are not banished. Pemberley is always your home. You *are* going to visit Aunt Matlock because I am ill equipped to teach a young lady. You need her help right now. Richard's sister, Helen, is your age and readying to meet society. You two can prepare together."

She bit her lower lip, tears welling again. "Will you tell them?"

"I must tell Richard; he is your guardian, too. We will decide what is appropriate for the rest of the family to know." His chest ached at her crestfallen posture. "You keep saying you desire to be treated as an adult. Grown people take responsibility for their mistakes. They do not hide from their errors, and they set things right with those they have hurt. Remember what Bradley—."

"Please, do not make me talk to Mr. Bradley!" She clutched at his waistcoat.

"Dearling, there is no choice." *I cannot let you become lost in your guilt as our father was.* "You must face all of us and see we forgive you. It will help you find the strength to forgive yourself."

"He must hate me!"

"That is not true, though you probably hate yourself right now." He tipped her chin up. "I am disappointed in your behavior. I expected more from you."

She sniffled and gulped back a sob.

He sighed as he contemplated his father's journals. *It is not what I envisaged from him either.* "We all fail the ones we love at times. If we cannot forgive and move on, what do we have left? To grow old and bitter? I do not desire to spend the rest of my days in resentment. Do you?" A sharp knock drew Darcy's attention. "Yes?"

Davis cracked the door. "Mr. Bradley, sir."

"Show him in."

Her eyes pleaded for mercy.

"Do not prolong this." Darcy held her arms and forced himself to glare at her.

Swallowing hard, she whispered, "Yes, sir."

A moment later, Davis entered, Bradley at his side.

"Good afternoon." Darcy tipped his head. "Would you care for tea?"

"Thank you, yes." Bradley smiled at Georgiana. "Good afternoon, Miss Darcy."

Her composure shattered, and she began to cry, hiding her face in her handkerchief.

Bradley crossed the few steps to her, exchanging weary glances with Darcy. Joints popping, he dropped to his knee beside her seat.

"Mrs. Cooperton made me see how horrid I was to you last night!" She hunched over her lap, her words muffled. "Please forgive me."

"Of course."

"I was so dreadful. You must hate me."

"No, quite the opposite, in fact."

She lifted her head, fixing her red-rimmed eyes on him.

"Your parents would be proud of you at this moment, as am I."

She blinked slowly, and her jaw went slack.

"It takes much to confess one's error. Be assured, I hold nothing against you." He nodded encouragingly.

Darcy crouched along the other side of her chair. "I am proud of you, too."

"Really?" She craned her neck to peer at him.

"Yes. Now, refresh yourself and go attend Mrs. Cooperton." With a kiss to the top of her head, he walked her to the door and sent her to request their tea.

Bradley settled himself in a chair by the fireplace. "If the shadows beneath your eyes are any indication, you slept very little."

"I dare say the circles under yours match mine." Darcy laughed, seating himself.

They squirmed and stared at each other until the arrival of a maid bearing tea.

"So, tell me of your evening." Bradley cradled his teacup.

Darcy took a long sip, his eyes fixed on the bookcase. "I needed my father's wisdom last night. I started reading his journals."

Bradley's cup clinked against the saucer. Leaning elbows on knees, he blew out a deep breath. "I am sorry."

"You knew all along."

"Your father trusted me with his confidences. I would not violate his trust, any more than I would violate yours. He intended to tell you at the right time." Bradley scrubbed his face with his hands. "He suffered much for what he did."

"That was evident in the many pages he wrote about his ignominy." Darcy's brows creased, and he looked at the ceiling. "I do not understand how such a thing occurred. When I left for school, he lectured me to keep myself under good regulation, so the shades of Pemberley would not be darkened—" He snorted, grinding his teeth so hard he thought they might break. "Clearly he knew better, but it did not seem to matter."

"Do not be deceived, it mattered, very much."

"But how could he?" Darcy sprang to his feet and paced across the hearth. "You did not condone ..."

"No, I did not."

"How many?"

"None. Let me put the question to rest. There were no others."

Darcy sagged against the mantle. A sigh of relief escaped, tension and strength both draining away.

Bradley heaved himself out of his chair and shuffled to the fireplace. "Come, since you already read your father's words, I will tell you the story as I know it." He laid a hand on Darcy's arm.

For several deep breaths, Darcy drew strength from his friend's presence. They returned to their tea.

"Your parents' match was like most of those in their sphere, a business transaction. Something happened during their wedding trip, though. They came to love each other." Bradley stared at the empty fireplace. "Sadly, adversity came against them very early in their marriage. In their first five years, they suffered no less than six miscarriages. With each, your mother fell into progressively deeper melancholy. Your father, still an impatient, young man, was unable to share her sorrows. They grew more apart after each loss. He hoped your birth would restore your mother's spirits."

Darcy peered at the tea leaves swirling in the bottom of his teacup. "I knew nothing of their pain. Neither of them spoke of it."

"These things are not openly discussed." Bradley shrugged. "His desires were not to be. Despite being safely delivered of Pemberley's heir, Lady Anne's melancholy descended in force. She withdrew from everyone, especially your father. His hurt quickly turned to anger. At length, she announced she would take you to visit her family at Matlock. He allowed her to go, hoping it would somehow ease her heart, though he was not pleased." Bradley exhaled hard and took his teacup once again.

"I find it difficult to even imagine these things. I did not think his temper resentful." Heaviness bowed his shoulders and dropped his eyes to the floor.

"It is hard to talk about him this way. To speak of the man he once was almost disgraces his memory. The man I am speaking of became the father you cherished. He took his mistakes and learned from them. Keep that in mind."

Darcy tapped his heel and grunted.

"The longer your mother absented herself, the more his anger grew. He began to wash away his sorrow in drink. Most nights he fell asleep in his study after far too many glasses of port. Needless to say, the estate suffered in those days. Thus, he brought in Old Wickham as steward."

The hair on the back of Darcy's neck bristled, and he grumbled loudly.

"The Wickhams had no children, despite their long marriage, and Lavinia Wickham longed for a child. One night, she came to the manor, looking for her husband. She found your father, in his cups. I cannot say for certain what happened though I know they entered into physical congress."

Revulsion overwhelmed him. Darcy jumped up and stalked to the window, throwing it open and drinking in the fresh air.

"Their dalliance did not last long. At the end, she carried a child, and Old Wickham was left to stand Moses.[27] He may never have recognized the truth."

"I am relieved it was short lived."

"Sadly, the effects were not. Your father knew Lavinia's child was his, and guilt consumed him. He sank into a dark place, darker than your mother ever experienced, barely speaking to anyone during that time. When he did, he could only focus on how he had failed all those around him: his wife, his heir, and his natural child." He joined Darcy at the window.

They gazed over the estate. Bradley's presence alleviated some of Darcy's tension.

---

[27] To stand Moses: when a man has another man's bastard child foisted upon him and is obliged to maintain it.

"Your father was a man of principles. In his anger and unforgiveness, he allowed his baser nature to overcome his principles."

"That is what makes this difficult to believe of him."

"He struggled with disappointment in himself." Bradley sat against the windowsill. "Your mother finally returned home and was a changed woman. However, he barely tolerated her presence; he was so eaten by guilt. On my counsel, he confessed himself to her, despite his fear she would leave him again."

"I cannot fathom what he said to her."

"Indeed. She felt his betrayal most keenly. Lady Anne could not accept what many wives tolerate with equanimity. Over time, she and I talked. She came to understand she had a choice: hold her bitterness for the rest of their lives, or forgive him and try to rebuild what they once had."

"She chose to forgive him." Darcy recalled his father's words. "He never understood how she did it. The grace she extended him gave him the will to continue."

"Her decision changed the course of all of your lives. They slowly rebuilt the love they had experienced early in their marriage. They worked hard to create a union worth envying."

Darcy raked his hair. "Now I am confronted with the same issue of forgiveness."

"Too true. Your father failed to forgive himself. His failure devastated him and left his natural son to pay the price as well."

Darcy strode to the bookcase, carefully choosing a journal. Opening it, he briefly read over the entry. "He said you told him a father disciplines the son he loves. Guilt, not love, was his driving force where George Wickham was involved."

"He did Wickham no favors by giving in to his demands while requiring nothing of him. If your father had forgiven himself his own mistakes, he might have handled Wickham more effectively."

"So now I am left to make recompense for them both." Darcy slammed the book shut.

"The father's iniquity is visited upon his children." Bradley trundled over to lean on Darcy's desk. "What will you do with the legacy he left you?"

He slipped the journal onto the shelf. "As much as I dislike it, I must forgive my father … and Wickham, too, lest I repeat Father's folly." Darcy's calm demeanor shattered, and he stomped to the desk. "How can I allow him to walk away? After what he tried to do to my sister, you expect me to let him go?"

After a long pause, Bradley replied, "I ask nothing of the sort."

"You will tell me the good Lord requires me to 'turn the other cheek' and ignore …" Bile burned the back of his tongue. He swallowed the urge to spit it out.

Bradley rubbed his hands together unhurriedly. "I said no such thing, nor will I."

Darcy gaped.

"Forgiveness means you release your right to judge him and return it to the One who judges us all. It does not mean freeing him from the consequences of his actions. Your father showed no love to his natural son when he failed to bring him up under discipline, and it has brought us to this place. Continuing in his ways will solve nothing. You have the opportunity to right the wrong against young Wickham. Forgive him, but let him feel the weight of his behavior." Bradley slowly met Darcy's eyes.

"You would send him to dance on nothing?[28]"

"Do his crimes warrant that fate?"

"No, they do not. Neither should he escape from justice."

"I agree. However, no easy answers exist. I think we should speak to Edwards."

"Richard, too. I sent for him last night." Darcy pinched the bridge of his nose, hoping to stave off the impending headache. "Cooperton should weigh in on this as well."

"There is wisdom in a multitude of counsel and no reason for you to try to do this alone." Bradley clapped his shoulder.

---

[28] To dance on nothing: to be hung

7 DO NOT WITHHOLD DISCIPLINE FROM A CHILD

To come a cropper. To be done over. To have a hearty choak and caper sauce for breakfast. Frummagemmed. Dance the Paddington frisk. Succumb to hempen fever. A hundred different ways to describe it all amounted to the same thing: tomorrow he would die. Darcy spoke against him at the trial, just as Edwards had warned. None came to his rescue. They all walked away. He remembered a laughing voice scoffing, "He will go to the noose sniveling, no doubt." Fear snaked down his spine, cold and quick, coiling through his guts.

He scanned the filthy cell, wrinkling his nose at the odors wafting from the latrine bucket. "Darcy turned against me. I thought he would be like his father. Edwards insisted I should not have tried to convince her to elope. Perhaps he was right."

He paced three steps to the barred window and four steps to the door. He could do it with his eyes closed now, three steps, corner, four steps, turn …

"Old Darcy promised me …" His voice rasped, a phantom noose tightening around his neck. "No. He guaranteed nothing. 'Take orders, the Kympton living is in my power to bestow.' That is what he said. 'Take orders.'"

Bitter fury bubbled up, and he kicked the rough stone wall. "Bloody hell!" He clutched at the searing pain in his foot and stumbled.

The grimy straw rushed at him. He landed with a thud that left him as breathless as the gibbet would. Clambering up, he noticed someone had mercifully provided wine. He knew not who. *Darcy probably … the bastard.*

"At least I will feel nothing," he muttered, taking a deep draw off the first, potent bottle.

He soon finished it, but the pleasant buzz and creeping numbness he expected did not come. Bewildered, he took the second, quickly polishing it off. Still no comfort. A third and a fourth offered no effect. He reached frantically for yet another only to be cruelly interrupted.

"Enough. Time to meet your maker."

Hands bound behind him, the ragged ropes cut into his wrists. His heart raced, knees threatening to buckle. Forced steps … six … seven … the jeering crowd distracted him. He lost count. The motley group, many drunk themselves, shoved food into their mouths enjoying the spectacle.

"They will watch me decorate the sheriff's picture frame[29] for their morning's spree.[30]" His guts roiled, and he tasted vomit in the back of his throat.

Soberly, far too soberly—*Why am I not drunk?*— he regarded the man who already stood at the nubbing cheat.[31] The floor dropped with a groan, the rope creaking under the weight. The condemned man's bare face knotted into a grisly death mask.

Moments later, a painful shove between his shoulders, and his feet were carrying him to the gallows. Throat constricting, he panted faster and faster, knowing soon he would breathe no more. The coarse rope bit into his neck, tightening, strangling his final thoughts. The blood roaring in his ears obscured words spoken behind him. The floor opened below him …

Wickham's head snapped up, and he searched the moonlit room. Realization dawned; he was still in the cottage, bound to the hard chair, Edwards's men to either side. They glanced at him and returned to their infernal chess game. He wheezed in labored gasps, his clothes soaked and stinking of fear.

Four chessmen were captured and "check" called twice before his pulse slowed and breathing eased. Three times now, sleep had brought this same dream,

---

[29] Sheriff's picture frame: gallows
[30] Spree: party of pleasure
[31] Nubbing cheat: gallows

each growing more vivid. The floor had not given way before.

Sweat he could not mop away burned his eyes. Bitter bile etched his throat. *This is all Darcy's fault. He did this to me!* He struggled impotently against his bonds, their cutting hold reminding him of the noose in his nightmares.

Sanderson glared at Wickham, lacing his meaty fingers and popping his knuckles.

He ceased his struggles and shook damp hair from his forehead. *Father told me I would be topp'd[32] unless I changed my ways. He saw this coming!*

The front door squeaked opened and heavy footfalls resounded. *Boots, expensive ones.* Wickham squinted, listening. *I must speak to Darcy. If I apologize to him, he will surely end this farce.* He dropped his chin to his chest, exhaling sharply. *I already dreamt he refused to listen to me, saying no apology mattered any more.*

Sounds from across the cottage intruded into his consciousness, drawing his attention to a vaguely familiar voice. Straining for a glimpse, he managed to distinguish the shadows on the wall and imagine those in the room.

"Where is he?"

Richard—no, he is Colonel Fitzwilliam now. What is he doing here? Wickham squirmed. *Darcy means to force me into the army?*

---

[32] Topp'd: hanged

"My men have him bound in the next room." Edwards's unique form obscured the other silhouette. "Do you care for coffee, sir?"

"You gave me a barbarous expensive habit, introducing me to the stuff!" Fitzwilliam's figure emerged in distinct profile when he laughed. "I would gladly take a cup."

Edwards moved out of view and returned bearing two mugs.

The aroma drifted into the dining room, souring Wickham's stomach. He swallowed the urge to retch.

"I sent a man to Manchester to investigate Wickham's debts." Edwards's shadow pressed a mug toward Fitzwilliam.

"Why bother? Theft is a capital offense. Give him to the sheriff and be done with the business."

He means for me to ride the three-legged mare![33] Blood drained from Wickham's cheeks. Dizziness drove out all other sensations. He screwed his eyes shut and shook his head, vainly trying to cast away the vertigo.

"I am surprised. You are too good a soldier to overlook possible advantages in case he hops the twig[34] somehow."

"As if that would happen under your guard, Major." Fitzwilliam took a long draw off his coffee. "A simpleton could tell he would come to this. Why Uncle Darcy kept feeding the cur's demands, I fail to understand. His generosity surpassed his good sense."

---

[33] Ride the three legged mare: to be hanged
[34] To hop the twig: to run away

"Indeed, I cannot fathom how his judgment failed him there."

"He left Wickham a legacy that should have been his gateway into a respectable life, yet he squandered the whole thing. If I had behaved as he ..."

"You would not be ready to retire to a place of your own soon."

He is to purchase an estate? Wickham clenched his jaw, growling softly. He bit back the epithets dancing on the tip of his tongue.

Fitzwilliam's shadow banged the coffee mug against the table. "How does he believe he, the godson, should be entitled to more than me?"

"The younger *son* of a peer."

"Uncle Darcy provided him as much as many younger sons receive! Education, money, introductions—and he has nothing to show."

Deep creases lined Wickham's brow. ... *as much as many younger sons receive* ... A cold chill slithered up his spine. *Fitzwilliam is right. He did, but, somehow, it did not seem so then.*

I wonder ... he was exceedingly generous. Might I be his son? What a joke! He chewed his chapped lips, playing out the possibilities. *No, even I could not convince them of such a thing. Old Darcy's reputation, his character, they all forbid the possibility. Besmirching his name will only seal their resolve against me.* An unfamiliar hopelessness blanketed him. *Did I go too far?*

· • ·᠗ᡅᢙᡣ᠂ • ᠂ ᡅᢙᡣ᠂ • ᠂ ᡅᢙᡣ᠂ • ᠂ ᡅᢙᡣ᠂ • ᠂ ᡅᢙᡣ᠂ • ·

The freshness of the morning air was just giving way to the day's more pronounced warmth when Darcy and Bradley met. Neither man had slept well, knowing the solemn task facing them.

"Colonel Fitzwilliam has already gone ahead?" Bradley asked, coming alongside Darcy.

"Yes, he needed to confer with Major Edwards."

Bradley looked at him quizzically.

"Richard still calls him Major, just like his men do." Darcy chuckled. "It may not be proper, but it fits."

"Too true." A crooked smile lifted the corners of his lips. "I find myself calling him 'Major' on occasion myself."

"Like when he decides to lead a hunt?" Darcy guffawed briefly and lapsed into silence. He listened to their footsteps crunching on the gravel. "I remember Father putting this stone in place. This footpath used to be quite muddy, and Mother would get cross at him tracking mud all over the freshly cleaned floors."

"She was most particular about her tile." Bradley winked.

Several steps further and Darcy paused a moment and kicked the gravel. Several pebbles skittered off the path. "Who else knows?"

"I believe no one does, though I think Edwards suspects the truth."

"What do I do? I prefer to honor my father's memory and not bring this to light, yet I hate disguise." He slapped his palm over his mouth and rubbing his jaw.

"Does the identity of Wickham's father change the severity of his transgressions?"

"I suppose it makes his imposition on my sister worse."

"Does his parentage change the consequences he should receive?"

"You teach the Good Lord is no respecter of persons. If that is true, only what he has done matters, not who he is."

"Will Wickham benefit knowing the truth of his paternity?" Bradley stopped walking and faced Darcy.

Darcy tried to continue past him, but Bradley caught his arm and held his eyes. Darcy muttered something indistinguishable, attempting to edge around him again. But the vicar quickly maneuvered into his path.

"Enough!" Darcy groaned. "Knowing would cause him to grow more angry and bitter against us all." He stared into the morning sky and rubbed at his temples. "Did Father ever give you any idea if he wanted to acknowledge Wickham as his natural son?"

"He did not say, yet that in itself is revealing. He spoke of telling you and asked my advice as to how, but never mentioned divulging the matter to Wickham. I believe he had no intention of it."

"I suppose you are right." Darcy blinked in the sunlight. "I must be true to my father's wishes as best I know them. I will say nothing."

They walked into a shady patch of trees that bordered Lady Anne's garden.

"How did she do it?"

"Do what?"

"Forgive him? He … with the wife of his steward! How could she forgive, seeing the proof of his indiscretion ever in her house?" Darcy looked off towards the rose garden. "Good Lord, she encouraged us to play together, to be friends!"

"Your mother was a woman of uncommon strength, but the task was far from easy. There were days she it took all her fortitude to speak to him." Bradley pulled a full blossom closer and drank in the fragrance.

"How?"

"She made a choice. Our Savior gave himself as a sacrifice in payment for our sins. Each day, she chose to let that sacrifice be payment for his sin against her." Bradley paused a moment. "It was never easy, but, with practice, it became less difficult."

"So just a choice, a simple choice?"

"A choice, yes, though not a simple one."

"Father regained her trust so easily?"

"Not at all. To forgive, releasing her bitterness and pain, was the work of a choice, sometimes repeated over and over each day. Restoring the relationship was another matter entirely. Your father worked diligently to show himself a man worthy of trust. Do not be confused. A tremendous effort on both their parts went into making things right again."

Darcy stooped to smell a cluster of pink roses, drawing them close. A blossom shattered under his touch. He fingered the soft, fragrant petals before allowing them to float to the ground. They resumed their trek.

A short time later, they joined Edwards, Richard, and Cooperton in the cottage, around the plain dining table. Wickham sat at the far end, secured to his chair, between Elmer and Sanderson.

"Darcy!" Wickham shouted.

"Enough, Wickham! There is nothing I want to hear from you."

"You must listen—"

"Silence!" Darcy stomped to Wickham's side, color rising on his neck.

"Stand down, Darcy!" Edwards ordered, shouldering him aside. He jerked Wickham's sweat-stained cravat loose.

"What are you doing? Stop!" Panic filled Wickham's eyes.

Edwards yanked the silk, allowing the length to tighten around Wickham's neck until the fabric worked free. He pulled it across Wickham's mouth and tied a quick knot. "We need none of your interruptions. No, do not scowl at me so. Since you cannot keep your remarks to yourself, you will remain quiet." He returned to the head of the table.

Darcy watched as Wickham's characteristic arrogance evaporated and defeat bathed his countenance. Dark circles shadowed fear-filled eyes.

Does he finally understand? Darcy snorted softly, recalling their conversation in his study. *I doubt it.*

"Ordinarily, I would call this meeting in a public place. But, in deference to the affected family," Edwards nodded at Richard and Darcy, "we are handling this privately, for now at least."

"We are much obliged." Richard dipped his head.

"We must determine Mr. George Wickham's fate. All here, save the Colonel, witnessed the evidence of Wickham's theft from the Darcy residence. The stolen property's value and the fact he burglarized a dwelling make this a hanging offense; however, I am not permitted to pronounce judgment on a felon. He must go before a proper judge for sentencing."

"It is likely his sentence will be commuted to prison or transportation." Cooperton grumbled unintelligibly under his breath, and cast a black look in Wickham's direction.

"Not for theft in a home." Richard tapped his fingers loudly. "Judges are not inclined to mercy now that numerous great houses have been burglarized."

"He did not break into the house." Bradley said. "People fear being attacked in their own homes, thus the capital penalty. He was an invited guest. Does that mitigate the crime?" He glanced at Darcy.

Darcy scoured his face with his hands and nodded.

"You would let him walk free?" Richard pushed splayed hands against the table and pitched forward.

Wickham's eyes brightened, and he gazed expectantly at Bradley.

"Absolutely not." Bradley raised an open palm.

He slumped in his seat.

"The merchants in Manchester put together a writ of debt against him. We might surmise his thievery was the act of a desperate man, one likely to grow more dangerous with time. I would expect he is apt to burgle again, or worse." Edwards's fingers drummed his glass.

Wickham shook his head violently and protested through the cravat. No one attended.

"Death is too good for him," Cooperton muttered over his teacup.

"What is that you say?" Edwards leaned in.

Cooperton trained his angry glare on Wickham, who blanched. "He stole the lives of two of my maids."

"He is not a murderer," Darcy whispered, forehead creasing.

Wickham nodded vigorously, stopping when Darcy scowled.

"I never said he was," Cooperton snapped.

The men were silent for a long time.

"Prison?" Edwards steepled his fingers and examined on his ragged fingernails.

"Wickham's tongue is far too glib. He would soon talk himself out of the place." Richard propped his elbows on the table.

"I agree. His life should not be easier than the one he left my maids to live." Cooperton leaned on his fist, rubbing his knuckles against his thin lips.

"You are not considering the army?" Richard sat bolt upright. "I have had men like him under my command ..."

"… and I would not wish him on any company!" Edwards exchanged a somber look with Richard.

"He has enough friends to buy himself a commission. An officer's life is too easy for him." Cooperton said.

"The Navy?"

All eyes fixed on Darcy.

"Despite everything, I need to respect my father's feelings for Wickham and provide him the opportunity to redeem himself." Darcy avoided their gaze.

Silence enveloped the room. Wickham stared wide-eye and screamed muffled cries through the gag.

With a quick glance at the others, Edwards loosened the knot and freed him to speak.

"The Navy is worse than prison! They send the press gangs into the prisons to 'recruit' men to go to sea! Darcy, no, you cannot mean it. Surely you are speaking in jest, I learned my lesson—"

Edwards replaced the cravat though Wickham continued to shout muffled protests.

Richard bobbed his head slightly, considering. "There are no commissions to be bought. He is too old to serve as a cabin boy, so the only position open to him is a lowly landsman. He will have to work hard. No crew tolerates a slacker. Nonetheless, under a competent captain, he may do well enough for himself."

"A captain who would keep him shipboard," Cooperton said, "and who understands his history, one who does not tolerate his proclivities. That might do."

"I know such a man!" Richard's hand landed forcefully against the table. "Captain Rogers, he is just now taking a new ship and in need of men. I did him a good turn a few years ago, and he owes me a favor. He will take Wickham for me. Rogers is a fair man, though strict, and runs a tight ship."

"Some would say the Navy is a death sentence." Edwards addressed himself to Wickham. "Others argue it is a prison for those serving as landsmen. I can accept it as sufficient punishment."

Wickham's muffled objections fell on deaf ears.

"I will buy his debts in Manchester," Darcy said. "The merchants do not deserve to suffer. But his debts of honor are his problem alone."

Cooperton grunted. "And if he shows up without leave, you will see him in debtor's prison for those obligations faster than he can tuck tail and run."

Darcy blinked, clamping his lips together hard.

"So, gentlemen," Edwards extended open hands, "are we agreed?"

Slowly, each one murmured his approval.

"Have you anything useful to say, Wickham?" Edwards removed the gag.

Wickham gulped several times and stretched his neck. "This is utter nonsense! Tell them, Darcy! End this charade and release me. I give you my word—"

"Everyone here realizes your word is worth nothing." Richard sneered.

"This time I mean it. You will be free of—"

"Enough!" Edwards pounded the table and moved to replace the cravat.

"What would you have me say?" Wickham snarled.

"You may accept the pronounced sentence, or gamble with the judge." Edwards crossed his arms over his chest.

Wickham glared at Darcy. "Do you believe this honors your father?" The typical steel was gone from his voice. "He would let me go."

"Perhaps. I will not repeat his mistakes." Darcy chewed his cheek. "Many fathers obtain a place in the Navy for their younger sons. It is not remarkably different from what Richard's father did for him. You were his godson, Wickham; would he really do more for you?"

Wickham stared, but Darcy's resolve did not waver. His head dropped. "I am for the Navy."

"Have you nothing to say to the man you wronged?" Edwards nudged his shoulder.

Wickham opened his mouth to speak but shut it, twice. "If you release me, I will never trouble you or your family again."

"To plague another? I think not." Darcy snorted and rose. "I trust the arrangements to you." He bowed toward Edwards and turned on his heel.

Bradley followed him out, breaking into a jog to catch up with Darcy's long legs. "Have mercy on an old man. Slow down!" He braced his hands on his thighs and panted hoarsely.

Darcy paused, staring off at nothing.

Breathing more easily, Bradley approached him, but received no acknowledgement. He touched the sleeve of Darcy's coat. "You were most generous with him. Your mother would have been proud."

Darcy stood a little straighter. Pressing his lips hard, he struggled to hold the dam against the surge of emotions threatening to break forth. He turned to meet Bradley's eyes. "I had not considered her perspectives in all of this. I have been so concerned with honoring my father's memory, I never thought ..."

"You did what your father never could. You honor both their memories."

Words snagged in his throat. He forced himself to speak against the tightness, "Thank you."

8 A WIFE OF NOBLE CHARACTER

"Three more weeks, Rebecca!" Georgiana danced through her sitting room. "Can you imagine? Just three more weeks until my dashing cousin whisks us off to London!"

Rebecca laughed. "A few days ago you were sulking and crying about being banished from Pemberley."

"That was before I knew you were a part of my aunt's invitation!" Georgiana beamed and twirled around.

"Your aunt is an influential woman. I am honored to be included in her beneficence."

"You sound so stiff and formal! Promise me you are not going to be so starchy all the time we are away."

Rebecca giggled. "You know me better than that."

"Was Fitzwilliam not the most considerate brother? I am sure it was his doing. He understood how I dreaded going alone."

"Especially considering, he might have sent Miss Bingley to accompany you instead." A mischievous smile lit Rebecca's face. "I wonder how much of your glee relates to leaving her behind."

"I cannot believe you said that!" Georgiana's hands flew to her mouth.

"As though the thought did not already occur to you?"

"But I did not say it!" Georgiana curled on the settee. "Tell me, what was her visit with you like?"

"Oh, she was awful! The things our brothers say about the women of the *ton* ... she is the embodiment of them all!" Rebecca flopped into the nearest chair.

"That bad?"

"Truly!" Rebecca hid her wide grin behind her handkerchief. "Mind you, her manners and accomplishments were exactly as society expects."

"She is an excellent musician."

"Certainly, though she enjoys performing far more than is proper." She sniffed, throwing her nose into the air in a strikingly good imitation of Miss Bingley. "Her conversation left much to be desired. Her preferred topic was last Season's gossip. I got an earful of the horror of Miss T.'s poorly made dresses and Miss M.'s dreadfully conjugated Italian. She picked at and criticized all of her acquaintance. Of course, she was full of compliments towards you and me."

"Really?" She wrapped her arms around her shoulders. "Why? I cannot imagine that anyone could possibly meet her standards."

"Is it not clear? How could you miss something so obvious?"

Georgiana huffed. "What are you talking about?"

"She came out several years ago and is nearly on the shelf. Miss Bingley is desperate to find a rich gentleman husband, and either of our brothers will do."

"Oh no!" Georgiana sprang to her feet. "How terrible! She could be my sister. We must do something!"

What began as a small laugh grew until Rebecca was consumed by her mirth. She finally wiped the tears from her cheeks. "You cannot be serious!"

"I certainly am. Are you not concerned? Do you want to call her sister?"

"Of course not! I was relieved to see her carriage departing. Her brother though! What a lovely man, a perfect gentleman. I would be happy for him to stay again." She batted her eyes. "But not at the price of tolerating *her*. Our brothers are not fools. They can spot a fortune hunter at a hundred paces. They do not need our protection from the likes of her."

"You are sure?"

"Absolutely." Rebecca beckoned her back. "Now sit down and tell me of your aunt's letter. You said she already has plans for us. I want to hear everything. We must make sure to pack correctly lest we become fodder for Miss Bingley's newest gossip."

Three days later, Darcy watched the carriage bearing Georgiana disappear down the road to Dunmore. Miss Bingley's company had proven too much for her, and she begged for the relief of a visit to her friend. He would have joined her himself had his obligations to the Bingleys not prevented it. With a touch of resentment, he returned to the house and caught strains of music. The intricate melody, one of Miss Bingley's signature pieces, only magnified his frustration.

What am I to do without Georgiana to entertain her? She refuses Mrs. Reynolds's company and instruction. What happened at the Coopertons? He hurried to his study, giving firm directions not to be disturbed.

The mantle clock chimed the dinner hour far too soon, and the event, without his sister to act as hostess, fulfilled his expectations of disaster. Relief finally came when Miss Bingley begged a headache and excused herself. Darcy wasted no time in retreating to his sanctum with Bingley.

"A lovely supper, Darcy!" Bingley settled uneasily into a chair. "It is a fine thing Caroline retired early tonight. We have had little opportunity to converse freely." He focused on the fireplace, avoiding Darcy's gaze.

"True." Darcy stirred the fire and sat down.

"What is troubling you? Your preoccupation is difficult to ignore." He looped his hands over his knee and leaned forward. "I pray this is not over my sister."

Bingley raked his fingers through his hair. "I realize she said some very untoward things tonight. Perhaps I should try to curb her tantrums more directly. I feared it would cause a worse scene."

"Her resentment of Mrs. Cooperton baffles me." Darcy puffed his cheeks and blew out a long breath.

Bingley jumped to his feet and strode to the fireplace. Shoulders sagging, he supported himself against the mantle. "I wish I knew how to control her better. She was abominably rude, not just here, but at Allynden as well! The way she fought and criticized Mrs. Cooperton—"

"I know Mrs. Cooperton only wanted to help her. I cannot fathom —"

"Caroline convinced herself Mrs. Cooperton deliberately plied her with false tales regarding the expectations of an estate's mistress to discourage her from … from …"

"Setting her cap at me?"

Bingley winced and nodded. "Yes. I fear I put the notion in her head when I told her you two were much alike."

"I still cannot conceive of how you arrived at that conclusion." Darcy heaved himself up and joined Bingley at the fireplace. "Really, Charles, I mean no offense, but what were you thinking?"

He sighed and picked up the poker to jab the fire. "I do not know. You warned me often enough that I speak too quickly and do not mind what I am saying. I should have thought more carefully before I said that to her. Those few words from me caused her to conclude she would be Pemberley's next mistress."

Darcy shuddered. "In your letter you asked me to——"

"Say no more. Listening to Caroline rant to Mrs. Cooperton, 'Mr. Darcy would never place such expectations on his wife!' was enough to convince me of my error." He drew his hands down his face, groaning. "Caroline left Allynden declaring she would prove Mrs. Cooperton wrong, hence her lovely disposition with Mrs. Reynolds today—oh I cannot apologize enough! Then tonight, you had the *audacity* to agree with Mrs. Cooperton. I am sorry. At times, I fear she is beyond all control."

"Perhaps we need to seek Lackley's advice on the care and management of sisters. He seems the only one among us who is managing well!" Darcy laughed. "So tell me, were Cooperton and Lackley of assistance to you?"

Bingley returned to his seat. "Both of them were true gentlemen and offered me generous support. Lackley showed me what goes into running an estate. I never appreciated how much work land management entailed!"

"You thought to purchase a place, and it would run itself?" Darcy shook his head slowly. "You are not the first to say so. I warn you, employing a steward to do the work for you is not an easy solution. Those who do so are often disappointed in their profits. I am certain an estate must be run by its master to truly prosper."

"Your friends and their ledgers agree."

"The idea overwhelms you?"

"Exceedingly." Bingley stared at the ceiling. "I think I should begin with a smaller place and lease first, so I might move into this slowly."

"Cooperton's advice?"

"Precisely, though I expect you would give me the same counsel."

"Yes. The three years of my father's illness allowed me to gradually take over Pemberley, learning from him and his steward. I am grateful for that time. I would not want to suddenly take over a large estate." Darcy paused, staring into the crackling fire. "Did his solicitor have any prospects for you?"

"He did indeed!" A boyish grin slowly spread across Bingley's face. "A place called Netherfield Park near the town of Meryton in Hertfordshire. It sounds like a good prospect on which I could cut my teeth. Will you come and tour the grounds with me? I would feel much more confident having your opinion."

Darcy laced his fingers and balanced his chin on his knuckles. "Will Miss Bingley accompany you?"

"No." Bingley chuckled at Darcy's immediate sigh of relief. "I told her, if she did, I would expect her to act according to Mrs. Cooperton's instructions. She decided to return to her friends in London, wanting nothing to do with 'servants' tasks' as she calls them."

"That will be to your advantage, I think. The country is not like town. If you alienate your neighbors …"

"I understand. Louisa, my other sister, has agreed to act as hostess, assuming I take the place. She is engaged to marry Mr. Hurst, who is currently doing business on the continent and will not return for some months. I am pleased to tell you she does not share most of Caroline's views."

No Miss Bingley? Perhaps this is worth considering. "It has been more than three years since I took time away from here. The business of spring planting is all but finished …" He tapped his fingers against his lips, contemplating. "A change of scenery is in order. If you are willing to wait until my cousin returns to escort Georgiana to London, then I will go with you to investigate this Netherfield Park and whatever Hertfordshire offers."

* • ᑫᕍᑫ᠂ • • ᑫᕍᑫ᠂ • • ᑫᕍᑫ᠂ • • ᑫᕍᑫ᠂ • • ᑫᕍᑫ᠂ • •

Ten days later, Darcy and his steward toured the far eastern fields that had been left fallow. The sun crawled along the sky and reached its cloudy zenith before they finished their consultation. *They should return soon. Please let it be today.* He sent his man into Lambton to arrange meetings with the solicitor and the banker for the coming week and then opted to take the longer path home. Figures in the distance caught his eye, transforming into familiar silhouettes. His breath hitched, and he galloped to meet them.

"New stallion, Darce?" Richard asked, pulling his bay alongside Darcy's chestnut mount.

"He is. I hope to improve my stables with his bloodline this year." Darcy glanced over at Edwards who urged his horse closer. "What news do you bring?"

"I never knew you to be so impatient!"

"Richard, do not test my forbearance. A fortnight—"

"Not nearly that long." Richard guffawed, turning aside to gaze at the manor house in the distance. "The deed is done."

Edwards moved in tighter. "You might say the entire operation went off with military precision."

"I find that difficult to believe. Nothing involving *him* is ever so easy." Darcy rolled his eyes.

"Ye of little faith! Do you deem us unworthy of your trust?" Richard kicked his horse into a trot. Edwards followed.

Dust from their horses' hooves left Darcy sneezing behind them. He pressed his stallion to catch up. "Just tell me!"

"Rogers's ship, *HMS Redoubtable*, should have already departed Portsmouth with Wickham aboard. Life will not be easy for him. Though, if he survives, he may have something to show for himself." Cold satisfaction crept over Richard's face. "His comeuppance is long overdue"

"Before you ask," Edwards said, "I left Elmer and Sanderson behind to ensure Wickham was on the ship when it sailed. I expect a letter confirming his departure in a day or so."

"What of Wickham?" Darcy scoffed. "Kicking and screaming the entire way?"

Edwards's eyebrows rose. "You expected something else?"

Darcy shook his head, snorting to cover a laugh. "Thank you both for all you did for my sister and me." *Wickham too, perhaps.*

"It is no more than the Darcys have done for me," Edwards replied. They reached a crossroad where a smaller path joined the main road.

"Would you join us for tea?" Darcy asked, turning his horse toward the small lane that led into the woods.

"If you will excuse me, I must decline today. My steward has business waiting for me." He saluted. "Not to mention, I wish to check the post!"

They all laughed and Edwards galloped away.

Darcy and Richard rode through the tree-lined path to the manor in silence. Once at the house, they ran into Bingley in the foyer.

"Excuse me, Darcy." Bingley stumbled, trying to dodge the unexpected presence of his host. "I did not see you there."

"Perhaps you need spectacles, Bingley." Richard grabbed his shoulder and steadied him. "Darcy is no small object."

"Thank you, no." Bingley straightened himself and adjusted his cravat.

"Going somewhere?" Darcy asked.

Bingley grunted and frowned. "My sister took to her rooms, and I need to have a bit of *tête-à-tête* with her."

"Ah, I see. We will be in the office if you care for sanctuary after your conversation." Darcy watched him tug his coat sleeves and trudge upstairs. He nodded Richard toward the study. "Coffee? Tea? Brandy?"

"Brandy … definitely brandy." Richard lowered himself into an overstuffed chair.

Darcy filled their glasses and leaned against the desk. "Tell me."

"I am unaccustomed to enduring prattle, so listening to the ungrateful noddy's[35] yammering was all but unbearable." He pressed his temples, grimacing. "Yet, just when I was ready to put his cravat to better uses, he would stop and, for fleeting moments, appear thoughtful. Perhaps the time at sea will give him an opportunity to think."

Darcy stifled a snicker. "It might be the first opportunity in his life for reflection."

"Rogers keeps his men shipboard. Only his officers are given shore privileges at port. Wickham will be denied many of his usual diversions. Seamen are a different breed and tolerate little, especially from the landsmen. I doubt his golden tongue will grant him any favors at sea. I expect him to find a rude awakening."

"I hope it comes." Darcy sipped his brandy.

"It will be no fault of yours if it does not. You gave him the chance. What he makes of this opportunity is his own doing." He scraped his palm along his stubbled jaw. "Who knew Georgiana was so naïve?"

---

[35] Noddy: fool

"I am glad your mother agreed to take her for the next few months. Georgiana needs preparation for her coming out. Clearly I do not comprehend what a young woman requires." Darcy dragged the back of his hand across his mouth. "I failed her."

"Do not judge yourself too harshly. You cannot dismiss her willfulness as your fault." Richard glowered for a moment, softening under Darcy's dejected mien. "She requires a woman right now. A man can only do so much." He savored the fine liquor. "Mother was delighted to extend the invitation to Miss Lackley, saying, 'She will be a brilliant role model for Helen and Georgiana, so poised and proper a young lady, and with excellent prospects, too.'"

Darcy snickered at his impersonation of Lady Matlock. "How open-minded of her, considering the Lackley's roots in trade."

"Indeed. I admit, sometimes she surprises me; however, *your* motives interest me more." He parked his elbows on his knees and leaned in.

"I cannot speak for Aunt Matlock's intentions. I will be honest, though, and confess Georgiana's happiness was not my sole purpose."

"I expect you find Miss Lackley's company awkward without your sister present?" He winked. "I see the fawning way she looks at you, and I imagine you do not welcome it."

"She is a sweet girl, with a good dowry, who will make an excellent match—for someone else. Miss Lackley is too young, a child still." Pushing himself off the desk, he began to pace the room. "I do not wish to offend Lackley; nevertheless, his sister is not for me. He does not encourage her toward me. Even so, I fear the suggestion would arise soon enough. In London, with your mother and Georgiana, she will enjoy the presence of young men who are more suited to her charms."

"These last three years have only intensified your serious and brooding ways. I would not have thought it possible."

Darcy glared. "Do not go there. You cannot appreciate what it was like …"

"I have seen my fair share of death, cousin. I might understand more than you expect. My time on the continent was no grand tour."

Deflated, Darcy rested against the window casing. "You are right. It is far too easy to forget. Forgive me."

He nodded curtly, eyes following Darcy's pacing. "The marriage market repulses you."

"It feels even shallower, now." Darcy paused at the bookcase holding his father's diaries.

"What changed? Have the matchmaking mamas conspiring with their conniving daughters devised new schemes to lure you in?" Richard's cynicism echoed off the windows.

"The *ton* is as it ever was." Darcy ran his fingers down the black leather spines of the journals.

"Bradley?"

"In part, I suppose." Discontent filled him, forcing his feet to move again. "I have been reading my father's journals. I miss him."

"I admired him, you know." Richard stood beside him, near the window. "He was a man of few vices. I never saw him in his cups, or looking at any woman but your mother. I cannot say that of many, even within our own family. My brother ..." He snorted. "Uncle Darcy was a model of gentlemanly behavior."

Darcy averted his eyes, fearing what Richard might read in them.

"Your parents' relationship was a rare and admirable one. Not one in a hundred, I think, experiences such a bond. Mine surely do not. So you set your sights on the unattainable? I fancy you want what you read about in those journals?"

Darcy opened his mouth to speak but closed it again. *I will not dishonor his memory. You do not need to be acquainted with the depths of his imperfection.* "I read of my father's failings from his own perspective. My mother was a source of wisdom and strength to help him overcome them." He walked over to the small table and refilled both their glasses. "You are right. I do want that kind of marriage."

"If you were Pygmalion, you might fashion her yourself." Richard arched an eyebrow, just the corner of his lips rising. "You may have to—I fear your mythical creature does not exist among the *ton*."

"What I desire is not valued by society. The lady I seek is unlikely to be found in the London crush."

"Indeed not. Perhaps you should begin scouring the rocks and hills of the countryside to find her." He chortled and burst into full out merriment when Darcy grumbled deep in his throat.

"I want a woman of principles who is willing to live by them, not by the whims of society. So many lives are connected to Pemberley. I need someone who understands that burden and who is prepared to carry it. Someone who is ready and able to be a helpmate to me like my mother was to my father."

"That is a tall order. I wish you luck finding so unique a lady. When you do, be sure there is a sister who will take an old soldier like me."

Darcy sputtered out his brandy. He mopped his mouth with his handkerchief and tried to ease the burning in his nose. "You mock me."

Richard's glass clinked softly as he put it down. "You think I jest? I am most serious. If you find your precious gem, I require she has a sister, elder, younger, no matter which. You must promise to write me from wherever you are, and I will come to claim her." He took up his drink again and finished it quickly. "Do not look at me like that! I am entirely sincere. I share your revulsion at the *ton's* matchmaking and fortune hunting. A lady of principle and virtue would suit me."

"Even a poor one? I was led to believe you reserved your attentions for women of substantial means."

"I have acquired my fortune and am ready to retire. It is in my power to afford a gentlewoman with little dowry. However, were she to be rich, I would not reject her because of her wealth!"

"An eligible young lady stays here now." Darcy winked.

"That horrible Bingley woman?"

"How can you speak so of my guest? You barely had three words with her." He crossed his arms over his chest.

"Two more than I needed!" Richard frowned, his eyes narrowing. "Jesting at my expense! I thought you had become more dour! How could I misjudge you so? Here, I trust you to find me the woman of my dreams, and you direct me to that harridan!"

Laughter bubbled up and Darcy smirked. "I will be quite happy to make an introduction."

"Enough! I apologize for all those introductions I made for you in the last two seasons. Nevertheless, none of them warrants an introduction to *her!* " He grinned, his peculiar lopsided smile, and tasted his brandy. "You must realize I am honest when I say ..."

"I promise, if I ever find my mythical creature, there will be a sister, several in fact, and I will bid you come and choose among them." Darcy snickered wistfully. *If such a woman exists.*

A soft knock preceded Bingley's entrance. With a glance, Darcy knew, and he poured another glass of brandy. Bingley fell into a chair and took the liquor. "I do not often say it, but I needed this!"

"I have seen men return from battle looking less harried than you!" Richard chortled.

"Perhaps you would like to skirmish with my sister?" Bingley tossed back the remainder of his glass.

"I would just as soon stick to the French, thank you."

"I assume that you will be departing for Hertfordshire soon?" Darcy crossed his legs and leaned into his chair.

"As soon as I can make the arrangements to send Caroline to London." Bingley snickered. "Do you suppose she could walk from here?"

"A forced march to town?" Richard barely choked out the words. "In sarsanet no less!"

The men roared until tears flowed.

"Now that image is indelibly impressed on my mind." Richard slapped his knee. "But, Hertfordshire? Why go to that market town?"

"Cooperton's solicitor pointed me to an estate there. Darcy's going to survey it with me."

"Searching for an estate? I shall be doing that soon enough myself. I am interested in hearing what you find." Richard lifted his glass. "Here is to good hunting."

Darcy raised his drink. "Good hunting." *I wonder if mythical creatures might be found there as well.*

DON'T MISS THE EPILOGUE

GEORGE AND ANNE DARCY'S STORY

A WEB EXCLUSIVE
AT

GIVENGOODPRINCIPLES.COM

9 SPECIAL PREVIEW

THE FUTURE MRS. DARCY
GIVEN GOOD PRINCIPLES VOL 2

Early Spring, 1812

It is a truth universally acknowledged that wherever men in red coats gather, foolish young women follow.

The militia regiment had arrived in Meryton a week ago, and it was high time for them to be introduced to the community. The mayor, Sir William Lucas, well known among his neighbors for his love of good society and a good meal, liked nothing better than to make introductions. His parlor provided the ideal location for the officers to make a good impression.

Lydia bounced and chattered more than usual during the ride to Lucas Lodge, a difficult thing to accomplish with all six Bennet ladies squeezed into the coach at once. Elizabeth had offered to walk and allow them additional space.

"No, Lizzy, I do not want you seen arriving on foot. Besides, your petticoats would be six inches deep in mud by the time you arrived. I insist you ride with the rest of your sisters." Mrs. Bennet finished with a flourish that meant the discussion was indeed over.

When the coachman finally handed her out of the carriage, Elizabeth hid her sigh of relief in a discreet, ladylike cough. Mama shepherded Kitty and Lydia ahead of her and scolded them for being so long at their dressing tables that the Carvers had arrived before them. Jane and Mary followed at a less anxious pace. Elizabeth lagged behind and shook out her skirts, more to enjoy a brief moment of silence than to repair the state of her gown.

Mr. Bennet dismounted his horse and passed the reins to the driver. "Perhaps you ought to offer to ride Bessie next time. You would escape the carriage, and your petticoats would remain clean." He straightened his top hat and offered her his arm.

"I hardly believe Mama considers the smell of horse more fashionable than muddy skirts." She took his elbow and leaned her head on his shoulder.

He patted her hand. "If you say so, dear."

The modest parlor of Lucas Lodge, papered and painted in the style of years gone by, brimmed with guests. Sir William stood at the center of the room. His welcoming voice and laugh, both a fuzzy *basso profundo* rumble, filled the air. Young ladies surrounded him: Kitty, Lydia, his youngest daughter, Maria, and the fashionably dressed Carver sisters, Martha and Rachel.

"I dare say this will be a memorable season for Lydia." Mr. Bennet turned to Elizabeth with a raised eyebrow. "First, the Carvers take Netherfield." The corner of his lips rose ever so slightly. "I never thought to encounter another girl as silly as your youngest sister, and lo, not one, but two move into the neighborhood. Now the regiment camps among us. Any more excitement and she will be in danger of apoplexy."

A wry smile crept over Elizabeth's face. "Mama appears quite content. I daresay, Lydia shall be able to bear it as well." Her brow quirked, and her eyes flickered toward Mama in the far corner of the room, deep in conference with Lady Lucas and Aunt Phillips.

"You should go on, have your share of introductions while I partake of Sir William's library. He recently received a new collection that I am most anxious to examine." He winked and walked away.

She scanned the room.

Mary stood near the pianoforte and talked with Mr. Pierce, the hawk-nosed curate whose velvet voice left young ladies sighing. Her eyes glittered, adding volume to her quiet smile. Mary pulled her hair back a bit too tight and wore her collars a bit too high for most young men to pay attention to her. Only rarely did gentlemen take the time to speak with her. Mr. Pierce's popularity ensured others would soon interrupt, so Elizabeth sought other company.

Jane and Charlotte waved her over. She edged her way around the parlor.

"I thought I would not be able to make it across the room." Elizabeth sidled in close to Jane and Charlotte to clear the way for a scurrying maid. "Sir William has outdone himself tonight."

"You there, mind your step." Mr. Carver jumped aside. The punch glasses he carried in either hand nearly spilled.

Elizabeth cringed. Mr. Carver's nasal voice raised the hairs on the back of her neck. He moved like a portly heron, head bobbing forward and back, feet lifting a mite too high as he walked.

"Here." He pushed a cup at Jane's shoulder.

Jane blanched a bit and screwed her eyes shut. She blinked several times and turned to him with a paper-thin smile. "Thank you."

"I detest clumsy servants," he mumbled into his cup. "Gah, this is too sweet." He smacked his lips.

"I will inform my mother, sir." Charlotte nodded amiably, but a tiny "V" shaped crease deepened between her eyes.

"Be sure and do that. I wish to sit. Miss Bennet?" He took Jane by the elbow and guided her to a pair of chairs near the fireplace.

"At least his sisters are more agreeable." Elizabeth huffed. Her nostrils flared ever so slightly.

"Jane finds his company pleasant."

"She bears it well enough, I suppose, though I detect no symptoms of peculiar regard in her demeanor."

Elizabeth pulled herself up and peered down her nose to ape any one of a number of women they both knew.

"Lizzy!" Charlotte snickered behind her hand. "He will hear you."

"Not likely. Look how he glowers at his sisters."

"They stand far too close to those officers." Charlotte's lips pulled tight. "At least Lydia and Maria keep a more proper distance."

Elizabeth rubbed the back of her neck. "I do not expect that to last very long."

Charlotte chewed her knuckle "No, it will not." She pointed her chin at the pianoforte.

Lydia skipped toward Mary, three lieutenants and an ensign in her wake. Kitty led a wave of young ladies behind them.

"I expect Mary will play a dance soon." Elizabeth wrinkled her nose.

"I thought you liked to dance."

"You know I am fond of dancing. It is having my toes trod upon I dread." Elizabeth glanced down and wiggled her foot towards the soldiers' boots. "Imagine the attack those hessians might wreak upon one's slippers."

Charlotte pressed the back of her hand to her mouth. She trembled with the effort to contain her amusement.

"Look at them, tripping over themselves to ask our sisters for a dance. Such grace does not bode well for a jig." The corner of Elizabeth's lips twitched.

Mary played a few chords while Rachel and Martha Carver directed the officers to roll up the carpet. Elizabeth and Charlotte dodged other guests who hurried off the hastily prepared dance floor. The couples took their places.

Only Lydia's partner showed any sense of rhythm. At least the others laughed heartily at their own missteps. A good sense of humor was a most desirable trait in a man, and essential for a clumsy one.

Carver did not share their amusement. He sat beside Jane, a deep scowl etched on his face. She squirmed and scuffed her slippers along the floor. Her cheeks tinged pink, not the pale blush of pleasure, but the ruddy glow of discomfiture. Jane needed rescue, so Elizabeth set off on her mission.

"—I do not understand why a knight like Sir William hosts these ruffians. I could easily do without the whole lot of them," Mr. Carver muttered into his fist.

Jane acknowledged Elizabeth with a quick nod. "Sir William is a great lover of company. To overlook—"

"Stuff and nonsense." Carver flicked his fingers. "I will not condone their presence at Netherfield's ball next month. The regiment is most assuredly not invited."

"Are you not concerned with giving offense?" The color crept from Jane's cheeks up her temples and down along her jaw.

"A man may do as he chooses in his own home. You cannot mean to say—"

"Excuse me." Elizabeth tucked herself between their chairs to accommodate a woman of ample proportions as she struggled to get past them. "Mr. Carver, might I steal my sister away for a few moments?"

He crossed his arms and tore his eyes from his sisters to peer narrowly at Elizabeth. "Certainly." He rose, bowed to Jane, and stalked into a knot of twittering young ladies.

"I do not envy them." Elizabeth took his seat. "He is quite severe on the Miss Carvers. If his face becomes any redder, I fear he may do himself an injury."

"His concern for them is not so terrible." Jane peeked over her shoulder.

"Do you suggest other young ladies might benefit from…stricter supervision?" Elizabeth followed Jane's gaze.

Lydia sat amongst three spellbound lieutenants who listened to her chatter. She granted them all pretty smiles and coquettish gazes. Kitty stood a few steps away with Maria. Both exerted themselves to gain the attention of an ensign whose eyes were firmly on Lydia.

"Are you not at all concerned?" Jane asked.

"Papa is not alarmed."

"Mr. Carver—"

"You cannot please everyone, Jane. Mr. Carver is the sort of man who will always be dissatisfied with something. Since everything displeases him, why be concerned with any of it?"

"But—"

"No, he is a curmudgeon. Even Papa says so. Do not take his complaints to heart." Elizabeth pulled Jane to her feet. "Come, Sir William wants to make introductions. It will not do to be rude to our neighbor even for Mr. Carver's sake. If the officers are a bit boorish, still, what harm is there in the acquaintance?"

COMING JULY 2012

ABOUT THE AUTHOR

Though Maria Grace has been writing fiction since she was ten years old, those early efforts happily reside in a file drawer and are unlikely to see the light of day again, for which many are grateful.

She has one husband, two graduate degrees and two black belts, three sons, four undergraduate majors, five nieces, six cats, seven Regency-era fiction projects and notes for eight more writing projects in progress. To round out the list, she cooks for nine in order to accommodate the growing boys and usually makes ten meals at a time so she only cooks twice a month.

She can be contacted at:
author.MariaGrace@gmail.com.

You can find her profile on Facebook:
facebook.com/AuthorMariaGrace

or visit her website at
AuthorMariaGrace.com

GOOD PRINCIPLES
PUBLISHING

Made in the USA
Lexington, KY
20 March 2013